THE DESCENDANTS

DAWN OF THE VAMPIRE AGE

Aries Braeburn

FELIS HORIZONS INC • TORONTO

A Felis Horizons Book
This edition published by Felis Horizons Inc., Toronto.

This book is the first installment in the *Vampire Age* series by Aries Braeburn.

www.vampireage.com

Interior layouts & cover designs by Felis Horizons Inc., Toronto, graphic design and corporate identity division.

www.felisbooks.com

ISBN 978-0-9813702-1-7

First Edition: 2010

TO

EVERYONE

WHO

GAVE ME REASON

TO KEEP TRYING

WHEN I WAS READY TO GIVE UP

PROLOGUE

Nine years ago. I had spent days scrambling through the crowded human city streets with an urgency I had become all too familiar with. I was looking for a place to hide as if my life depended on it--but it wasn't my life that was on the line; it was the life of a human boy named Luke.

Luke had been trying to track me down all week because he was utterly convinced that he had found true love at the wise old age of eleven. Well, I was only ten so that made both of our life experiences, at the time, equivalent to the blink of an eye in my species.

We met on an old bus in the boroughs that rattled as though it were falling apart by a second. The only thing louder and more obnoxious was his imposing friend, who had approached me on his behalf. I noticed Luke had been staring at me for more than twenty minutes already and I also knew he had been pleading, in urgent whispers, for his friend to just let it go and leave me alone. Apparently, he had already concluded in his own mind that I wouldn't be interested in him. Little did he know, his whispers--though drowned out to human ears by the ambient noises--were as audible as panicked human breaths, to a vampire.

By the end of the night, I had persuaded Luke to offer me enough of his blood to satisfy my thirst but not nearly enough to put his life in any danger. As I pulled my fangs out of his neck, I could see plainly in his eyes that I had persuaded him a little too well. In the days that followed, he was relentless in finding clever ways to track me down.

I had been sympathetic to humans since I was a child but it was the first time the food had been so determined to see me again.

Two days after the initial feeding, Luke managed to locate me in the heart of the city and almost pressed against me as we stood together in a crowded subway station. I had newfound respect for the determination that his species is capable of, given the proper motivation--respect, and maybe a touch of fear.

"I love you, Verdana," he muttered.

"That's not even my real name, you know." I made all efforts to avert my eyes and spoke as quietly as I could manage.

"It doesn't matter. I just know from the feeling in my stomach--I know what it means. I know how it sounds but-- We belong together...forever."

"Or maybe you're just lactose intolerant or something. Look, I really don't want you to get hurt, okay?"

Despite all my efforts, nothing could drown out the over-blown romantic ideas flowing through his head about us spending an eternity together. A casual midnight snack turned into my first lesson in human mating psychology at its most obsessive.

He insisted that he didn't care if he might get hurt. Unfortunately, it wasn't his feelings that needed protecting; I knew that, with my ability to control my thirst at the time, I had to avoid my food entirely after the initial feeding. Otherwise, it would be an epic battle between my juvenile vampire willpower against centuries of evolution in hunting instincts--and I already knew the only possible outcome had I allowed that to happen at ten years of age. Still, nothing convinced Luke to give up on his idea of us as an eternal couple.

So I roamed the city in search of an elder to plead for a small favor. It wasn't--and still isn't--common for city vampires to ask for favors from strangers in our own species. I just figured I might make a few personal sacrifices and do whatever it took to save the life of the innocent human I had fed on.

That Friday evening, I took notice of two people standing on the rooftop of an office building on Wall Street, just a block east of the cafe I frequented then. They were too far to smell or hear clearly, but I squinted and used my near-perfect ten-year-old night vision to see that the younger-looking male had his fangs bared--not in a threatening fashion, but in a stressed effort to speak his mind, possibly even attempting to calm the human.

A moment later, I watched in horror as the human male dove more than forty floors to his death on the sidewalk before me. The sight had haunted my dreams for years to come.

Later, I met with the male vampire who, as it turned out, spent hours trying to talk the human out of committing suicide. I knew immediately that any vampire willing to put in that kind of effort to save a human life could understand my motives.

His name was Adrian. There was an unusual variation in the vampire signature in his scent but that quickly flew out of my mind as I noticed his eyes glistening as he smiled gently at me. It triggered all sorts of childishly romantic fantasies that would fill my mind. I couldn't tell how many years older he might have been, since all adult vampires look to be in their prime for centuries. He could have been anywhere from twenty to a few hundred, for all I could tell from looking at him.

Either way, I decided that there was no way fate would have me meet my eternal mate the way we had met. I was just grateful that Adrian agreed to help me protect the life of the human child.

We staged a confrontation at the south shore of the island in an area where I knew that Luke would be likely to have an unobstructed view of us. Adrian and I pulled punches and just-close-enough-to-look-real fingernail swipes. It all appeared real and brutal enough to put any human stuntman or professional wrestler to shame. At times, we made contact but neither of us would cause any real damage; the most we did was give each other a gentle, high-speed massage with as much facial acting ability as we could muster up at that age.

As Luke emerged from an office-turned-apartment building across from Battery Park, Adrian pretended to end my life with a final bite into my neck. I contorted my neck as much as possible with what I would like to believe was a chilling level of realism. In reality, the bite was little more than a human-style kiss--topped off with a light scratch caused by the tip of his fangs.

I dropped to the ground and laid motionless with my eyes opened by just a slit, just enough to see through while still appearing closed from a distance.

Apparently, Luke was completely convinced that the strong male vampire standing before him had murdered the love of his life. With tears building up under his eyes, and adrenaline pumping through his veins, he charged toward Adrian in an emotionally driven fury. For a moment, even I believed he might have been able to hurt the vampire...but it wasn't to be. Adrian over-powered the human child and wrapped his hand around the boy's throat, effortlessly.

"What I did here tonight was a favor to you," Adrian told Luke. "This demonic girl marked you for death. Now, run along and--"

"How would you know?!" Luke managed to scream through his vampire-palm-compressed throat.

"We can sense these things among our own kind, child. Now run along and live your life."

Upon being released from Adrian's grip, the boy turned with eerily carnivorous eyes and growled, "You murdered my true love. I don't care who or what you are. One day, when I find a way, I'm gonna track you down, and I'm gonna tear you to pieces."

Adrian and I parted ways that night and I nearly forgot about him in the nine years that passed since the incident. I never even got a chance to tell him my name. I believed in fate then...maybe someday, I will again.

CHAPTER 1

oday, you could say I live a very different life. I can feel the sharp, cold tip of a dagger as it digs into my back. It doesn't quite break skin yet...but I can feel it pointed straight at my heart. I take in a deep breath and fill my lungs with thick, heavy smog-filled air. A faint glow emanates from behind my light green eyes--every little crack and pebble in the skyscraper's shadow is visible to me now.

Sniff. It's human.

There's not another soul for an entire block as far as I can see, hear or smell. It's just me and whoever's holding that lethal pointed weapon on my being.

Up till a year and a half ago, I probably would've turned around and drained its entire circulatory system in two minutes or less. My appetite was enormous--it was a genetic curse but I've learned to cope. I've got other priorities now.

From my childhood until I was fourteen years old, I was the vampire species' equivalent of an animal lover. I hated to see humans die or suffer so I fed only for sustenance and left the prey alive when I was finished. You might even say I was friendly and caring to them if they would behave. Naive and childish at the time, I dreamt of a future where we could keep domesticated humans as pets but training them to be obedient is easier said than done.

My human-loving habits became a bit of a problem when I fed on the locals--the adolescent and adult males would get deeply infatuated with me after I had fed on them. Some would try to track me down and follow me until I was forced to finish them off. Each of those creatures were utterly convinced that they had found a deep connection, a sense of true love.

Naturally, tourists became my food of choice. Unlike the locals, it wasn't all that practical for most of them to stay in the city for longer than their planned vacation. And even if they had the resources to stay, many would find a way to go back to their lives abroad. I could only imagine the impression I gave them of our city but it seemed better than mass slaughter.

When I turned fifteen, I met and dated a male vampire who also fed on tourists under the bright lights and news tickers. By then, I was the one who was convinced I had found true love. He wasn't the brightest bulb in the pack; he was one of the many barely-educated city-raised vampires who believed in all the human myths about our kind as inherently evil beings...that is, until the day he accidentally touched a cross and realized that he wasn't melting. Still, he was my first love--and probably my worst love.

He called me a B.E.T.H.--a derogatory term that apparently originated from the rural vampire communities upstate. It stands for *Babies for the Ethical Treatment of Humans*. Eventually, I caved in and joined him on a brutal two-year hunting spree. It wasn't as offensive to my beliefs as hunting for sport, but I still paid for my indulgence in spades. It caused me to gain more than thirty pounds...and then he left me.

Today, at nineteen, it's been a year and a half since I've fed on a single drop of blood. I don't know much about our metabolism but I know I'm losing weight as slowly as a human would--and I'm still not even close to where I want to be.

Yeah, I'm not where I want to be.

I guess you could take that in more ways than one. After all, I'm still single, breathing some human-killing smog, and feeling a knife pointed straight at my heart. I don't think anyone would want to be where I am right now.

"Look, I really don't have any money or jewelry on me, you can check for yourself," I announce to the human behind me. My hands reach for the sky with palms wide open...as if it really makes a difference.

A soft, light, little girl's voice responds, "Don't play dumb, Valeska. You know exactly what I want from you."

"Wait...what'd you just call me?" I crinkle up my nose, partly because she just confused the hell out of me--and partly because there's a vomit-like odor that seems to come and go.

"Valeska. I know who you are."

"My name's Iryna and last I checked I didn't know

any armed robbers on a first-name basis." I'm not sure she believes me.

Now, the weapon breaks skin.

I guess she doesn't believe me--or she's going to settle for a different robbery victim than she expected. Either way, figuring that out isn't my first priority right now.

In the blink of a human eye, I push forward, turn, swing my arms at a speed that creates a blazing arc in the air, grab the knife with one hand, and...

Pop!

The cupped palm of my other hand snaps onto a firm grip on the throat of my attacker.

The dagger clanks against the edge of the gutter.

It all happens before the human could even blink her eye but I could see and control every detail of the entire motion. It's second nature to me after living most of my life in this metropolis. I've learned more of these skills than I'd like to.

It's just a child, a little girl--no more than ten years old, I think to myself. What kind of world do we live in?

Seeing my glowing green eyes, she's probably asking herself the same thing. It's a good bet I'm giving her nightmares and therapy expenses for the rest of her life.

She heaves and struggles and kicks to no avail. I smile in temporary victory. My grip is just firm enough to keep her from running, but not so hard that her life is in any real danger.

It's also the first time the culprit knew to aim straight for my heart. Maybe she just got lucky or I must be getting a little rusty from the insomnia. The blade of the dagger drilled into my back by about an inch, maybe more. It hurts like no other species could even imagine when people so much as poke the heart region a little too hard.

The skin, flesh and bone around the hearts of vampires are the most sensitive parts of our entire bodies. It's probably nature's way of letting us know when the most vulnerable part of our bodies is in danger. I've heard some vampires take advantage of this for pleasure too...but for lonely singles like me, all we've got is a half empty cup there.

The point is...what this little human girl just did to me felt like three hundred paper cuts right on the tip of a human finger.

She's an adorable little creature though, I'll admit that. Maybe this is how the humans feel when they see a cuddly baby animal before they go home and eat slices of its relatives for dinner.

She stares into my eyes and looks strangely surprised.

The pungent odor gets stronger. It's got the vampire signature in its scent but the rest of the smell isn't pleasant.

Rigid, cold hands squeeze my arm like a vice. I feel a pair of eyes staring at my wound, analyzing it more than normal. "You will not survive to be three hundred years of age."

"It's that deep? I was guessing about an inch."

"No, I am referring to your weight, dear."

I turn and glare at the blunt stranger. "You always so freakin' rude to strangers you just met?"

The woman shakes her head. "The correct term is concerned. Rude would be your use of a juvenile human-American euphemism--particularly before an elder."

I shake her hand off of my arm and the back of her hand brushes against my elbow. Powdered makeup rubs off and reveals her natural skin: glossy and ever so slightly translucent, even a little crispy to the touch. Otherwise, she has the appearance of a human woman in her thirties if it weren't for her uncovered skin texture. With her tall, statuesque figure and classical features, she probably attracted a lot of quality prey in her day. To other vampires, it's not the appearance that gives her away--as long as she has make-up on--it's her scent that does. Even I've encountered enough of our elders to recognize that smell.

Anyway, the old vampire is probably seeing things. Contrary to human mythologies, I can see my own reflection so I know I'm not nearly thin enough right now.

The clever little human capitalizes on my obvious distraction.

She punches my elbow, wedges out of my grip, and then drives her foot into my breast plate with a crunchy impact of sneaker sole on bone. She then rolls over and snatches the dagger from the ground and dashes away with a surprisingly long stride.

I guess she does a lot of running in her line of work. It must be the adrenaline--that wonderful fight or flight hormone that sets off my glowing night vision and allows humans to lift cars.

She's got a barrel of guts, that little animal.

I try to chase it but I'm being held back by something rigid and aged--I have no clue how old she really is but she's definitely been alive for more than a few centuries.

And the old vampire just couldn't resist tossing in

some more criticism on my life. "Do not feed on the little ones; there are healthier foods for weight control if that is what you seek. The average human child sorely lacks the necessary nutrients to sustain our kind...and the flavors are atrocious."

"I wasn't going to feed on her, lady. I was out here minding my own business and that little girl tried to rob me with a knife. Look what she did to my back--I'm the victim here!"

She nods and smiles, like I'm some sort of test subject. "Fascinating, the psychology of your type--"

"My type? What's that supposed to mean?"

"City-raised vampires, dear. I have studied both humans and vampires for centuries, and the regional differences are simply astounding."

"Well robbers are robbers, and now they're starting young. So she needed to be taught a lesson--human or vampire, city or rural, I don't care."

"It was not a robber; it was an unsuspecting prey that fell for your bait."

I squeeze strands of my hair between my fingers and sigh. "Weren't you even listening? I didn't bait her. She was the one who attacked me."

"I am speaking of the natural bait, child: Our physical resemblance to their species, despite our vastly evolved biology. We naturally lure them to their deaths simply by appearing to be harmless members of their own species. It is nature."

I turn to walk away. "It's the thought that counts, right? So she was still an armed robber."

"I would like to offer you a--"

I speed up. "I don't want your help and I never asked for it. So stop following me."

The elder follows me... silently.

For the next half hour, I choose random routes around the city in hopes of either boring or distracting her until she leaves me alone.

She doesn't.

She just follows me and follows me through dark and smelly and crime-ridden without seeming to hesitate. She calmly watches me every step of the way.

That's fine.

She may be centuries my senior, she may even see me as a baby in the scope of our species' lifetimes-- but I've got nineteen full years of experience in pure stubbornness. Based on her accent--especially her pronunciations of the vowels--chances are I know this city better than she does. I can ignore her for longer than she can stand to follow me around this island.

Maybe she's trying to help me overcome my psychological issues or maybe she wants to study me like some vampire guinea pig. I don't care much either way. I'm not asking to be fixed, least of all by some stranger who can't keep her opinions to herself.

That wonderful stop-walking hand flashes before us, cursing me to the fate of standing next to the annoying old vampire for at least a few more minutes.

We stand in pure silence. Not even a word.

All I hear are the dry hacking coughs that echo through the human-built jungle. It used to be a crowded city, even over-crowded, with all kinds of healthy prey from around the world to feast on. Today, healthy prey is few and far in between.

No one knows what happened exactly. Everyone has an opinion but no one has a solution.

The thick smog started to engulf our skyscrapers about two years ago. The humans swore they were coming up with new ways to emit less carbon, to be more environmentally friendly and all that--but all I've seen them develop lately are new respiratory diseases. Our species has stronger lungs, but it's becoming a shortage of quality food--for the ones who still feed at all, that is.

I can barely see farther than a block ahead of myself, even with night vision all tensed up.

I glance at the giant glowing red numbers of a digital clock across the street. It's three thirty in the morning--we've got a few more hours before direct sunlight hits the city. I wonder how far the glossy-skinned woman will go before she leaves me alone.

Maybe I'll hit a bar and lose her there.

Who am I kidding? I haven't been to a bar since I stopped stealing IDs from the prey. In all likelihood, I'll be spending my sleepless daylight hours at the public library. It's one of my favorite places to avoid direct sunlight during the day when my insomnia kicks in--and that's pretty much every day lately.

It probably sounds like the least exciting and glamorous thing a city vampire girl could do all day, but that human history stuff is one addictive soap opera. Where else can I live vicariously through super-powerful beings, and then sit back and criticize their mistakes as if I'd have done better?

The little white walking man signals us to cross the road.

I step over the gutter and--

A car speeds by. It comes within an inch of hitting

my foot. Vampire drivers around here--they're reckless beasts. I hate them.

I'll lead the crazy old bat to the busiest road on the entire island. If there's one place in the world with enough humans to tempt her away from me, it's there. The quality's fallen off but it's still more in quantity than anywhere else in the borough. She's got to settle for something there.

I haven't been there in a while anyway.

We're bathed in the warm red glow of flashing light patterns, towering over-sized versions of retail chains, and scrolling tickers that tell you everything from stock prices to the number of burritos sold since 1982.

It feels like a homecoming--except it's more than just a little depressing seeing it the way it is now.

Back when things were still booming around here, more and more of the businesses were being taken over by vampires, in singles or pairs, running entire companies staffed with humans who knew they could either be yes men or dead men. The music, car horns, and subway trains provided some of the loudest and most constant ambient sounds in the world--and that was no accident. How else would our kind drown out the screams and grunts of all the hunting going on at night?

It was a vampire haven.

Rich, unsuspecting tourists would come from around the world to see the lights, pay for pictures of themselves, and dine on the criminally over-priced food. The most aggressive hunters would choose the best of the best to feed on, citing their subtle taste for exotic prey from abroad. Personally, it all tasted the same to me--I only fed on them for practical reasons when I did at all.

Today, it'd probably be a daily struggle just to find clean blood that doesn't trigger the gag reflex. There's one way I can rationalize my choice to stop feeding: it's an act of charity to the other vampires in the area.

Out of curiosity, I check my peripheral vision. Unfortunately, the elder's still following me and she's got a crooked smile on her face like she knows everything. I hate that.

A young couple on the opposite side of the street looks to be tracking a fit, healthy male prey about half a block ahead of me. I can tell they are because I used a variation of the same stalking pattern back in the day.

They've locked onto a rare find and they're about to share a romantic dinner together.

The female notices me. She probably thinks I'll compete for the kill; I slow down a bit to make sure she knows I won't.

To the humans, I live in one of the most social and connected centers of communication, from television to computers to banking networks. For vampires, this city is a disconnected center of chaos for hunting and doing business in singles and pairs only. Most of my reading comes from the human books, so everything I know about myself and my own species is from either trial and error or picking up bits and pieces of rumors overheard around town.

Lately, word is there are tribes forming treaties out in the rural areas. Maybe it's true, I don't know. All I know is that being single here is like walking up the down escalator--all the males just want a quick fix and all the females want to snap your limbs in two. And forget city friendships. For vampires of the same gender, it's always a competition for food or for a mate. There are no real friendships here, just a game where the first one who finds a way to screw the other one for personal gain wins. Humans play the game too but they play with words and numbers, not fangs and fingernails.

The ones who do find a good mate here are like lottery winners--and I'm watching two of them.

The female vampire ushers the prey into an alley between two glowing restaurants. The male follows.

I speed up to get a better view. The elder follows at the same pace.

Against a dumpster that reeks of leftover human-hunted meats and spilt grease, the male takes hold of the prey's head and...

Snap!

He turns it swiftly until its nose faces the same direction as its heels.

The couple exchanges a glance with shared-meaning smiles. They each run their sharpened fingernails down their palms. Blood fills the creases of their palm lines.

Their hands clasp and share their life force.

I've seen this before. It's a local vampire ritual for paired hunters but I can tell these two aren't doing it like some going-through-the-motions routine. I can see the love they have for each other--I can feel their eternal bond.

The male holds the neck of the prey open like a true gentleman, and gives the female the first bite.

And she bites down with fury.

She holds the still-warm carcass down with such

conviction, her shoulder blades jut out and her arms tense up. Blood runs down the alley, blending in with the pools of spilt cooking oils used by the humans to prepare their own prey.

Right now, any normal vampire would completely empathize with a human that watches from a distance as other humans feed on those slices of cow flesh and severed chicken limbs that they seem to love. But here I am, having mastered my discipline, standing next to an elder who only seems to be interested in studying my face.

I can't help but notice the female vampire's waist-- so thin and sleek.

Some people describe mine the same way but I don't know what mental malfunction is giving them those delusions. I only wish I could look as good as she does.

To add insult to injury, she's still feeding right before my eyes. How does she keep her weight down? Maybe she hit a jackpot in the genes department... Or she literally hit the jackpot and now she can afford surgery every few months.

I want to be her--in every way possible.

It's the life I dreamt of when I was a bright-eyed, naive little eleven-year-old. I thought the day would just come when my future mate would magically appear in front of me, and we'd both know. We'd tell each other, "I've been waiting my whole life for you," and start hunting together and living together. It'd be us against the world, with no one else to worry about and no one else to answer to. It'd be the ultimate bond, the ultimate trust--the city way of paired hunting.

I'm only nineteen years old and I've still got an

eternity ahead of me, and I'm pretty sure I can say that literally. But I can't even talk to other vampires anymore without pushing them away. Apparently, the only thing I can attract is a crazy, bitter old vampire who likes to observe and analyze me.

I glance over at her again to see if she's still there...and she is, unfortunately.

I let out a sigh and search the block for a human police officer. I find one. He looks healthy, even a bit juicy, but between my being off the feeding and his social status in this human-governed city, he's safe from my fangs. I'm sure even the elder knows not to feed on these.

Before I approach him, I quickly relax my eyes. The glow promptly disappears and my vision devolves into the same limited scope as human eyes.

"Excuse me, officer," I grab his attention. "This woman has been following me for like half an hour. I don't even know her but she won't leave me alone."

He turns to look at the elder, who manages a weak half-smile with her lips tightly shut. He asks, "Do you know this young lady?"

The elder takes a deep breath, and seems to convert it real-time into a deep exaggerated sigh. "Yes, officer. She is my daughter. She escaped from Bellevue. She has a history of memory loss and a severe case of body dysmorphia disorder. I have been trying to remind her of who I am for the last half hour so I could bring her back to the hospital." She begins to tear up a little. "I'm... I'm sorry, I just... I couldn't believe my own daughter couldn't even remember who I am."

He pauses for a moment. "I'm sorry, would you like me to call a--"

"It's okay, officer," the elder interrupts, "I can take it from here."

She turns to me and grabs my arm at full strength. She whispers, "I'm only trying to help you, dear. Now come with me."

The truth is she doesn't give me much of a choice. The woman's got the strength of an ox. I can feel the bruising as she pulls me down the street and weaves through the crowds.

"You are one evil old animal," I mutter.

"Are you ready to speak now, dear?"

"Fine... Do I really have a choice? What's so important about helping me that's worth all this?"

Her hold becomes a little less brutal. "I believe I have gathered enough information on you to be of help to you."

"You got all that from watching me walk for half an hour?"

"No. I have been studying the behavior of our species' city youths for some time. The expanding vampire communities on the West Coast are ushering in a new era for our species--a social era of cooperation and mutual support."

"So the rumors about the tribes and treaties are real?"

She nods. "It is my aim to help self-reliant city youths--especially those with worsening mental disorders--to better understand yourself, your species, and your place in this world."

"Why? What's in it for you?"

"Our species may soon face the same dilemmas as those faced by the human leaders. It is time to educate our youth to shape our future--when those of my generation become tired and weak. After all, you live in a city where the majority of the population believes that your kind is inherently evil. You face a constant internal conflict, knowing that your species' natural food source is also regarded as a social equal or even superior. Understanding is the key to survival--for all of us."

"What's so great about understanding? In the end, we all just feed, sleep, bleed, and... either get burnt in the sun or get staked... right?"

She cracks a smile. "Tell me, child... You expressed a specific hatred toward thieves when you encountered that young human. What is the reason for these feelings?"

With a roll of the eyes and a shrug, I tell her, "It's just armed robbers... It's not a big deal. I mean it's nothing personal if that's what you're getting at. I just hate armed robbers... and anyone who takes advantage of the weak for its own gain but they're the worst kind."

The elder seems to gaze straight into my soul. "I do not believe that is the true reason. Your feelings are rooted in something much more personal."

"It's true... And I don't wanna talk about it anymore."

"Alright then... May I suggest that perhaps the motives of this little animal were not rooted in greed?"

"Ugh. Why are you trying to defend that stupid little kid anyway?" With the stab wound on my back on display, I add, "Look what she did to me. Look."

"I am simply proposing a different point-of-view, to illustrate the importance of understanding. In times of prosperity, we all hold to our highest standards of ethics and morals. But when we are placed at the edge of survival, many of us would resort to unthinkable measures. Do you not agree?"

"Yeah, so we should all go around saying, it's okay to kill and steal and rob people? Oh, that person's poor so she can tear your heart out and sell it to the boss."

"No. You must understand so that you, as a generation, can empathize and help those who are in need--just as I see you are in dire need of help and have yet to seek it."

I lean in close to the elder. "I'm just fine right where I am. I didn't ask for your help, I didn't cry for it, and I certainly don't secretly want it."

"You seek companionship. You may deny it but every muscle on your face betrayed you while you watched that young couple feed in the alley. There is nothing you crave more than the bond they shared--yet you live in your comfortable self pity. You lie to yourself that every problem you suffer from is caused by genes, society, or those you've conflicted with--anyone but yourself." She pulls me in even closer and stares straight into my eyes. "Do you know why I understand your mindset, child?"

"...Why?"

"Because I have been there. I have been in your shoes, in the same pit of despair and living death-- up until less than a century ago. Now, come with me. Learn from me so you can step into my shoes... Or do not. It is your choice." She turns to walk away.

A storm of feelings and thoughts and fears run through but I know I've already made up my mind.

"Wait!" I call out and chase after the elder. "What's your name? You didn't even tell me your name."

She slows down. "You may call me Professor Marsden, young Iryna."

I stop. "How did you know my name?"

With a wink, she interrupts, "The first step to learning...is to accept that you do not know all that there is to know."

It takes me a few minutes, convinced she had some sort of extra-sensory perception, before I realize that she probably overheard my exchange with the robber. Or so I rationalize to myself.

CHAPTER 2

We embark on a five-day ride on a passenger train with the curtains firmly closed during daylight hours. It doesn't take our predatory senses to tell exactly which parts of the tracks are worn-out and which parts have been regularly maintained. Like everything in my life, I can block out the sights and sounds but I can't block out all the bumps along the way that are kicking me in the tailbone.

According to Professor Marsden, we're passing through the Central Regions of the continent. She seems a little surprised that I'd never been here. She explains that the region was the first to form tribes--made up of their most powerful vampire families in the early twentieth century.

All I know is, the doors are being opened and slammed shut again by the vibrations. I've heard construction crews in the city make less noise than this train.

After a while, we start to yell into each other's ears just to be able to talk.

"So how old are you?" I ask.

"I was under the impression that your question is as rude in your human city culture as it is in our communities."

"You're right. Yeah, it is. I haven't talked--like really talked--to anyone in like two years, so...it happens. Sorry."

She studies my face for a moment. "Relax, child. You will not look as I do for another two millennia, by my estimation." She winks.

"Whoa. So you're two thousand years old?" Like most vampires in the city, all I knew was that I'm *probably* immortal--except for stakes and direct UV light--but I had no idea how our aging works.

"I did not mention my age. I am simply estimating your rate of aging based on your facial structure and skin texture."

"How does it work for us anyway? Do we just look like thirty-year-old humans for a few hundred years?"

"Technically, our bodies age at approximately the same rate as the humans' for the first twenty to twenty-five years of our lives. Beyond that, their physical aging--their tissue degeneration--is far more accelerated and visible than our own. Most of our aging signs are quite simple to cover-up with basic powders and similar substances...but the odors are impossible to hide even with all of the fragrances in France combined. Believe me, dear. I am aware of this problem and have tried every method known to our species to circumvent it."

"So we're...not really immortal?"

"We may very well be, dear. There are absolutely no verifiable records of death by natural causes in our species. It is understandable that the human legends have told of our kind as immortals, though I would never consider the Homo Sapiens a reliable source of information."

"Doesn't the sun count as a natural cause? I mean, isn't that why the humans think we're inherently evil?"

"By that reasoning, water would qualify as well. Do your city humans consider drowning in water the same as death by old age? There is more water on this planet than direct sunlight exposure at any given time--perhaps they are inherently evil."

"Yeah, I guess they probably are."

"I was illustrating a point, Iryna. Neither species is inherently evil, only our individual choices could be. My research indicates that early humans were our direct ancestors. Our organs degrade slower, our bodies are stronger, and yet--based on empirical evidence from my travels--we share the same mental and emotional weaknesses." She looks directly at me as if I'm her latest study.

For the first time in my life, I'm getting an objective point-of-view on what it means to be a vampire. Maybe it's not the death and destruction that makes us special, but our chance to live longer and learn and experience more through the ages. Or so I'd like to believe.

Everything I've seen and everything I've studied has been filtered through the eyes of the humans who wrote the history books I read. Getting a first-person account from a woman who lived through it all is a like a complete re-telling of the same stories.

That settles it. I've decided to start my own volumes about my own experience. They won't be detached history books that summarize world events from a distance. They will be first-person accounts of my own experience as I lived it, written from memory with as much detail as my mind could retain...maybe even with a few contributions from others I might meet along the way. These volumes will be written entirely in present tense, so the future generations can re-live my experience as closely as my words could convey. If I succeed, it'll be the next best thing to being right here in my shoes just in case I end up witnessing some major world-changing event. Odds are nothing big will happen, but at the very least, future generations might get a taste of what it's like to be a twenty-first century vampire, who grew up in an entirely human-dominated metropolis, venturing to a rural vampire-governed community for the very first time.

All else aside, I'm glad for at least one thing at the moment: I've got the ultimate entertainment on-board for a history addict: a living, breathing elder vampire who's lived and experienced things I've only seen on paper. For the rest of the ride, I decide to take full advantage of my luck.

At first, it begins with a makeshift game of trivia.

The professor names a major historical event, and asks me to call out roughly when it happened. She gives me a margin of fifty years in either direction. If I get it right, she tells me a real-life anecdote from that very period in the history of the world.

Over the course of the trip, I get her to tell me about the night she met General Lafayette during the French Revolution; the time she encountered the first members of the Yakuza at the end of the feudal period in Japan, when they were border guards; and the night she landed in New Amsterdam--the Dutch colony as it was called before it was traded to the British and renamed New York. It turns out she did know the area--at least as it was in the seventeenth century.

Even if she may not have known--or even cared about--all the nitty-gritty details going on in the drama between the human nations, it's the personal moments that bring it all to life for me.

I could fill an entire book with her lifetime of experiences but I'm sure no one would have the patience to read it.

With an hour left before our stop, the professor gives me a gem of a story that I'll never forgot. It's not something I'd read about or something that's connected to some big world-changing event. It's just a story that will resonate with me for the rest of my life.

She begins, "The more you learn, dear... the more you will realize that you still know very little of this world." At first, I couldn't quite understand what she meant by that so she tells me a little story to wash it down a bit easier.

ARIES BRAEBURN

About forty years ago...

Miss Marsden sat anxiously in a room with the harsh glow of a fluorescent light that shined over her head. She watched the second hand on a clock tick away, loudly--vibrating her very sanity.

A headache began to set in so, with no remedy in sight, she simply tried to distract herself with anything and everything she could find. The subtle reflection on a security camera lens caught her attention first.

Unfortunately, that's not all that caught her attention.

Less than two feet away from her was a young couple, no more than twenty years of age, furiously locking lips--without a sliver of concern that they were in a public setting.

It wasn't so much the sight of it as it was the sound that got to Marsden--she couldn't decide which was more annoying, the mechanical ticking on the wall or the moist popping sounds of young human lips.

Finally, a young girl, dressed in a tie-dye top, calls out, "Ms. Marsden? You're next."

Marsden entered a dark room, decorated with posters of bright, reassuring crosses.

Behind a small wooden desk, a man greeted her with a firm, confident handshake. "Good evening, Ms. Marsden" his deep, booming voice echoed through the room, "I welcome you to my domain."

Marsden held in a laugh and quickly turned it into a bright smile.

"Take a seat," he annunciated her name clearly and gestured toward a block that could barely pass for a chair. He adjusted the collars of his glistening robe

before he reclined on his back-supporting throne-like office chair.

She noticed a shelf behind him--stocked with entire collections of guides to the supernatural and unexplained phenomena. They looked pristine, maybe even unread.

"I feel that you are an analytical person," the man suggested. "You work in a technical field--perhaps science or architecture. Maybe music."

"Yes, I do," she answered flatly.

He seemed to fixate his eyes on her, as if to read her more deeply. "You are single. Am I correct?"

"Yes."

"You feel helpless in a rapidly changing world. You feel alone and without companionship. You utterly despise public displays of affection."

"I was under the impression that I had paid for a psychic reading, sir," she replied with a sigh. "This is not a reading by any standards."

"Do you not believe?"

"Yes. I believe... that you have the ability to watch the security footage from the waiting room, and the ability to make guesses. Allow me to ask you, am I really single?"

"You are damaging to the aura of this room, Ms. Marsden. I cannot read the signs when you--"

"Alright, that is enough." Marsden stood up. "I helped to develop the technique that you are using, you fool. It is widely called cold reading and has been practiced for centuries. You have confirmed my suspicions."

Unscathed by her remarks, he replied, "Do not let your skepticism prevent you from enjoying a life of knowledge, Ms. Marsden. I will prove to you the accuracy of my reading."

Marsden held herself back and waited patiently for the man's next suggestion.

"I see... the sun," he announced with pride, "and the water."

"At midnight? Are you on some form of medication, dear?"

"I understand your cynicism, Ms. Marsden, but heed my words. There is more to this world than you will ever be able to prove with your science and logic and reason. There is a whole other world beyond, that you can only--"

She struggled to keep a straight face. "Yes, there is. So what exactly do you extrapolate from this vision of the solar star and H-two-O?"

He paused for a second, but only a second. Confidently, he replied, "You are a working professional. You work indoors--far too often, even. You have developed a host of vitamin deficiencies while your social life has been neglected."

She smiled at the analysis.

He continued, increasingly confident, "In fact, I believe it would be of great benefit to your health if you would spend more of the coming summer months on the beach, socializing outdoors, and enjoying the water under bright sunny weather."

Marsden burst out in laughter. "My mirror would have given the same diagnosis."

He paused and tried to recover, "Are... If you are suggesting that your own diagnosis would have concluded with the same information, then yes, you would have been correct and--"

"No, you fool. I would be wrong--as you are now, darling. Allow me to give you a piece of professional

advice--"

"Excuse me?" The man stood up to his feet with a bruised ego. "You, a woman of... a technical field, would like to give me advice?"

"No. I am offering my professional advice as an individual who recently discovered that I have been given the very gift that you pretend to possess."

"Are you implying that you are... also a psychic?"

She chuckled with arms crossed. "Also? No. I am not a cold reader although I am in support of the art as a form of entertainment. I have long considered myself a person of reason and observation--'a woman of...a technical field', as you so observantly stated. In all my years of studying your underdeveloped species, I have known that both of our worlds share a common trait: some embark on a search for truths while others, such as yourself, hold them back by exploiting people's ignorance. In doing so, you are retarding society's advancement in knowledge and understanding."

"How can you be so sure?" The man continued to grasp at straws. "As a woman of science, would you not admit to the possibility that--"

"You are capable of putting on a decent show, dear. Your showmanship and charisma is outstanding. I commend you for that. But I am also aware that a show is all that it truly is. You are now trying to instill doubt in my analysis. You are planting the seeds in my mind that maybe--just maybe--your act is in fact real. It will not work."

"Still," he adjusted his shirt again, "how can you be so sure? Perhaps I am actually capable of--"

Marsden leapt over the table and tackled the man to the floor. "This is why." She exposed her sharp fangs and moved in closer. "See, I am pale as you so aptly observed, but I highly doubt that increased social activities under the direct summer sunlight will be of any benefit to my health. Do you not agree now?"

"Oh my god! P... P... Please... Don't kill me."

"Calm down, child. If you listen to me and do as I command, you will survive this day. I am here in search of understanding, not of sustenance."

He began to tear like a fountain.

Marsden let out a sigh. "There is much I understand about you and your species. While I do not consider you an equal, I recognize your place as our evolutionary predecessors. And in studying your kind, I aim to learn more about--"

"I don't wanna die!" The man screamed at the top of his lungs.

Marsden slapped him with the power of a mule kick and continued, "I even understand your own particular techniques--you fish for cues until you confirm that a guess is worth pursuing. It is basic cold reading with a touch of charisma. I understand your penchant for this business."

"Look, lady. I'm just..."

With a finger over his mouth, she shook her head with a calm smile fit for teaching a child. "No, no, dear. If you interrupt so rudely again, I will be forced to suspend your ability to breathe... Now, we do not want that. Do we?"

He shook his head, obediently.

With a gentle smile, she continued, "Now, I understand your methods and I even understand your ability to convince your typical human customer of your legitimacy. What I cannot, for the life of me, understand is this: How exactly do you justify this act of deception to yourself? I must remind you that it is a deception for financial gain, dear. Do you not realize that your actions are the modern-day equivalent of stealing food off of another's table? How exactly do you sleep comfortably at night, knowing the effect that you have had on your victims?"

"I... I wouldn't call them victims, Ms. Marsden... I simply give people what they want. I give them hope."

"No, my profession gives hope... I teach. I show truth and discovery to new generations."

He took a deep breath to rack up a little confidence and replied, "What you give them is a picture of a black and white world. What I give them is hope that there's more to this world than your cold, logical facts about life and death. I give them the possibility of the beyond."

"That is where we disagree, dear." Marsden pressed her thumb onto the tip of her fang until a fresh, crimson bubble of blood emerged through her skin.

The man's fear quickly resurfaced. "W-- What are you doing?"

"You know," Marsden explains, "the sad fact is that people like you are the ones who truly believe in a flat black and white world. Deep down, you assume that there truly is nothing more to this universe than what little of it you already understand. That is why you feel free to exploit the ignorance of your peers without fear of consequence. Well, allow me to tell you from experience... there truly is more to this world than you are aware of, and you are only *aiding in adding to people's ignorance and lack of understanding of life."*

"But... Aren't you a scientist?"

"Yes. And, as a scientist, I form theories and then I test and explore the observable answers--to either confirm or disprove theories. Most of what you assume we do not believe in is simply just yet to be discovered or proven. Often times, when technology and resources permit, we stumble onto truths that the world previously believed impossible. There, darling, lies the true openness to a world beyond the accepted norms."

"I... I just do this for a living, ma'am."

"Relax..." Marsden watched with a sinister sense of pleasure as the blood on her thumb began to spread onto her palm. "You have already done your damage. Like every primitive misinterpretation of reality to have been passed off as so-called fact, you have already reinforced ignorance--and ignorance kills. It pollutes. Did you know that more than 90% of the world still believes that my entire species are mystical spawn of hell?"

"S-- So what are you going to... do to me?"

"I have a little psychic reading for you, dear," she grinned mischievously. "I see blood in your path. In fact, I believe it would be of great benefit to your health if you would announce, to all of your customers, that what you do--and have been doing-- is nothing more than an old psychological trick."

"B... But, I..." The man choked on his words. He couldn't stop himself from shaking.

Marsden fed a palm full of blood to the man like milk to a kitten. "If you refuse to do this for me, if you continue to sell your act as a true ability, then you will have something of an oxygen deficiency in the near future. And, believe me, once you have ingested a drop of my blood, I will have no trouble in locating you... Is that understood?"

"The truth is," Professor Marsden says to me, "I had no idea where the fool went the moment I left his place of business. I didn't care."

For all she knew, feeding him a dose of her own blood would do absolutely nothing to him. There was no scientific data in the disconnected and disorganized vampire scientific community back then. She just did it to give the man a taste of his own medicine: She suggested an idea that he might, just might, be in real danger if he continued to scam his customers. Even if he didn't really believe her, he would eventually give her the benefit of the doubt--the same reason his skeptical customers believed him and stopped asking for refunds. Ultimately, fear would overcome him if he continued to pursue his old ways.

Or so that was her intention.

But as she told me today, "the more you learn... the more you will realize that you still know very little of this world."

The lesson I got out of Professor Marsden's story is that the answer never lies in extremes.

For all those times we need to stay open-minded about new ideas, we need to be just as careful not to set ourselves up to be the next sucker to some con-man looking for a quick profit.

Maybe she had other reasons for telling me the story, but that's what I'm getting out of it right now.

"So did the man ever lie and cheat again?" I ask out of curiosity.

ARIES BRAEBURN

We arrive at our destination. The professor and I quietly join a long, slow-moving line of passengers-- mostly humans.

Just as I exit the train, I notice the little dark-haired girl who stabbed me in the city--at the back of the line.

Is she following me? Why would she? It doesn't make any sense to me. I don't have anything she wants.

I blink and look again. She doesn't blink at all-- she just stares at me from under her dark brown hair.

Her large round eyes seem frozen in time.

CHAPTER 3

As it turns out, the tribe that the professor belongs to controls a nice, green piece of forested land. I didn't exactly expect a city or even a human village, but at least a block of condos or a few small houses or something. Maybe I haven't seen the whole picture yet. She tells me they're part of the United Tribes of the West Coast, formed by one of those treaties I had heard all those rumors about--though she says their leader is a little more aggressive than she would have liked.

The school's not exactly a building either, or even really a school in the traditional sense. It's more of a local tutoring program in a designated part of the forest that the professor single-handedly operates. As primitive as it sounds, it's a giant step forward for our species.

For centuries, we've all had to learn on our own to become educated, either by real-life experience, or through loopholes in the human education systems. Quite a few would live for centuries before discovering that many of the human-originated beliefs about us were nothing but myths and fiction. Either way, some of the less ambitious ones could go through centuries without knowing a thing about what they really are, or what makes the world tick. Professor Marsden wants to change all that. She tells me she wants to set a new precedent, where young generations of our species could catch up on research about our own kind, our psychology and science, and the entire world around us--all within a few years under an organized system--the way a college-educated human is allowed to.

On my first day here, in less than an hour, I've already noticed a sense of community that I had never seen in the city.

In the half empty side of the cup, the air isn't one bit as clean as I expected it to be. In fact, the sky here is almost as smoggy as it was in the city. I'd hate to imagine it's a world-wide problem now though--the view of a clear, starry night sky used to be one of the only beautiful sights our species could enjoy in nature and we don't even have that anymore.

About thirty young vampires--all probably in their mid-teens to early twenties as far as I could tell--form a circle around the professor. Three girls are quietly giggling with each other, and another seems a little too relaxed to be fully awake. A group of boys are punching each other's arms with rowdy chuckles.

First impressions: I don't think I'd fit in here.

Falling back to old habits, I drop myself onto a willow tree and feel comfort in watching from a small distance. It won't win me any friends today but I definitely feel safer.

When the professor begins talking, they all quiet down and seem to listen so attentively.

The whole experience is just surreal to me--awe inspiring. There are so many female vampires, sitting within ten feet of each other...and they aren't all trying to break each other's limbs! That's a new experience for a city-raised vampire.

By a casual count, I'd say the male-to-female ratio is close to one-to-one in this class, but the males being friendly are less impressive to me. In my experience, it was the females in the city who were always the most competitive with one another. The males are only competitive when they lock onto the same potential mate, but even then, their fights are much less brutal and violent. Or maybe it's just all I experienced of it.

I wonder if all the rural tribes are like this. I wonder if we could take over the world if we all united and...

"Come in to the circle and join us, Iryna," Professor Marsden gestures to me like a game show host.

I shrug. "No, it's okay. I'm good here."

To be honest, the tree's starting to hurt my back. It's funny how social anxiety can trump physical pain. When I was maybe eleven, I probably would've sucked it up and jumped into the deep end but I've gotten worse and worse with my social habits over the years as a lone hunter. Being alone became a comfort zone.

Worst of all, the moment I glance at the circle again, I see that the entire class is now watching me. Some are curious, others are probably laughing on the inside. I shift a little and pretend the tree is as comfortable as a five-star hotel bed--or at least as comfortable as I'd imagine those would feel.

"Join us, dear," the professor insists with a piercing glare and a strange wink. "It would be greatly beneficial to you to form social connections in this community."

I'm not quite sure what she's getting at. Is she saying I'm an unsociable, nerdy, city beast? Well, she'd probably be right about that part.

In fact, she's entire right.

I came here to be a part of a community, to learn about myself, and to find friendships and relationships. I can't do that from ten feet away. It doesn't take a genius to figure that out--I'm just stupid enough to ignore my own reasoning.

I suck it up and hop up to my feet.

My ankles feel weak. My arms and legs begin to feel numb and tingly, and my heart beats like a drum. With knees ready to buckle, I enter the foreign terrain: a circle of socialized vampires.

Three of the females at the opposite end of the circle are quietly laughing and whispering with each other. It's probably about me. What's more nerve racking is that the rest of the class carefully observe me like some strange alien had just landed.

Finally, I take a seat. I cocoon myself into an imaginary ball and just stare straight at the ground.

It took less effort to chase a fit athletic male prey around the south shore of the city when I was eleven years old--and it took thirty whole minutes to catch that thing too. Maybe that's because the chase wasn't being watched and mentally critiqued by thirty fellow vampires who are no doubt criticizing every inch of my body in their minds by now.

Professor Marsden summarizes, "Confirmation bias is a phenomenon that causes us to interpret our experiences--and even our memories--to agree with our own preconceived beliefs. In other words, if we believe something to be true then we will naturally pick and choose just to find proof of it in reality... It is one of the many roadblocks for objective observers of reality."

A student raises her hand, "Do you think maybe it's our cultural influence from the humans that caused things like this?"

"That is an interesting idea, dear," the professor answers gently. "But confirmation bias is not a trait attained from values and beliefs. It is a natural response. Although it is true that we remain heavily influenced by the dominant human culture, it would only affect phenomena that come from the elements of culture--values and beliefs."

The professor turns to the rest of the class and continues, "Now, can anyone give me some examples of how and why the effect of confirmation bias can be a double-edged sword in a developed society?"

Just then, I notice him...a boy with dark hair, who looks to be about my age. He looks familiar...but maybe that's because his type is a dime a dozen, and as for the ones without fangs, I've probably fed on more than a dozen over the years. But this one does have fangs and, even in a class of about thirty, I can single out the vampire signature in his scent. He's definitely one of us yet I can feel his heart, heavy and crushed, as chemically obvious as if he were human. There's a deep sadness in him that's thinly veiled by some form of denial--I know that feeling all too well and I can recognize it anywhere.

If it weren't for his scent and mannerisms, I would even say he reminds me of Adrian, the vampire I had met when I was ten. The only problem is that he's sitting at the opposite end of the circle, right next to the three girls who were laughing and it looks like he's friends with them.

It couldn't be Adrian.

Still, I try not to stare...but I couldn't stop.

A girl sitting next to me interrupts my thoughts with a friendly nudge. I jump like a human who'd just touched a snake by accident.

"What's your name?" She whispers with a smile.

I smile back, figuring she saw me looking at the guy and probably wants to talk about him with me later. "I'm Iryna... Iryna Balmont," I whisper.

"I'm Angela, the one and only," she replies with a sinister smirk. It's a little intimidating but more likely intended to be a friendly glance of shared meaning--the kind I've always wanted.

I notice charcoal stains under her fingernails. I used to B.E.T.H.-feed on humans in the bohemian areas of the city before I moved on to tourists so I would recognize the mark of a charcoal drawing artist anywhere.

As my mind wanders into memories of food, I salivate a little. It's not exactly voluntary and I do have it under control, of course. It's just that sometimes the body reacts more to the mind's wandering than we would want it to.

Angela seems to notice this and somehow seems to understand it. She shoots me a smile. Maybe her appetite is acting up too.

That can't be good. What if she's trying to control her weight and--

"Iryna," Professor Marsden interrupts my silent *night-dreaming* session. "Do you have something to add to our discussion?"

I hesitate for a moment, flustered. It feels like an eternity while I search through my brain for a decent response.

My mind scrambles back into the topic of psychology and jumps onto the first answer that springs to mind.

I reply, "Umm...confirmation bias can block the road to advancement?" I imagine smacking myself upside the head. Someone, please hide me in an opaque plastic bubble.

The entire class seems to chuckle at my overly generalized and obviously pulled-out-of-my-ass response.

Angela just stares at me; I can practically feel her thoughts, all apologetic and caring, forming a shield over me. The only thing I wonder is: why would she even risk being my friend right now?

I smile back at Angela with a wink to signal: Don't worry about me. It's alright. I hope she gets it. She returns a caring smile. Yup, she got it.

Okay, I tell myself, *pull yourself together, Iryna*. It's time to sound smart. What do I have to lose right now anyway? I'm already an outcast to everyone else and I've got my only friend backing me--so it's all set in stone already.

I add with the most confident tone I can manage at the moment, "And it really is a double edged sword, professor. Sometimes, letting people believe in something keeps that belief a part of them for the rest of their lives--no matter how ridiculous it may be. If we convince our kids that cats secretly rule the world around the same time they learn that fire is hot, then every time a cat looks at them with those all-knowing eyes, the person would believe the cat is showing a sign of being a superior. Their belief is confirmed."

A few chuckles burst out around the circle. They probably think I'm an idiot but it doesn't matter now... I've come this far, so here comes more.

I continue, "Now, let's say we convince our kids that the world needs to be run with more sympathy for the weak, and more understanding of our neighbors, our peers. For the children who grow up to be the future leaders, instilling these ideas in their heads early would be as good a time as any. Deep down, they'll probably develop more empathy and have more interest in understanding. In the end, both of these cases--one being a load of crap and the other being very constructive for all of us-- are being reinforced by confirmation bias. So there, it's a double edged sword."

A dead silence falls over the entire circle for what feels, to me, like a million years. Everyone seems to be glaring at me. I think they hate me for showing off on my first day.

Finally, I overhear a girl with a fake orange tan-- one of the three laughers--whispering, "Like, why does she keep saying, our kids? Like she's ever gonna have kids." Her accent almost reminds me of people from my home town, but not quite--it's a strange variation where she pronounces her short vowels the way New Yorkers do but nothing else sounds like it. If I cared, I'd wonder where she's from, but I've heard enough.

Another of the trio, a monstrously tall, bleached-blonde, chuckles and adds, "What guy can even, like, kiss that thing without dying?"

The three of them and a few others around them are chuckling. He doesn't seem to be but he probably is on the inside. It couldn't possibly be that funny to anyone older than ten, but I'm starting to see where the centers of social power are around here. It's nice to know ahead of time--and I don't really care all that much...but now he is leaning in to Orange and whispering to her. That, I care about.

The two oh-so-funny comedian girls are now named Bleach and Orange as far as I'm concerned. I don't care what their real names are. They just proved to me that competition still exists in this community, and that's one thing I do have experience with.

Suddenly, I couldn't help but wonder: Am I really that unattractive to the other vampires here?

In all honesty, I don't know. Maybe I'm too short. Maybe I used too many big words in my answer. Maybe I should dumb myself down and use the word, like, every third word next time. That seems to work better than surgery here.

I look over at the one person I'd bet wouldn't be laughing...and I was right. Angela's glaring at those two idiots for me.

It's official. I found my first ally in this community.

"Can I break her arms and teach her a lesson?" I whisper under my breath to Angela.

"Leave it to me," Angela replies quietly with a

crooked grin. "Especially the tall one, I know I can take her."

Yup, she hates them too. And I immediately love her for that.

The truth is I wasn't being as figurative as she probably took it as. I was seriously asking if I could. If this was in the city, I would literally hunt those girls down and it'd be a perfectly normal thing to beat them to a pulp. I guess that wouldn't be socially acceptable in this community though.

The professor continues, "Returning to the topic at hand, Iryna has raised a very well thought-out and intelligent argument."

I don't dare to look but I'm sure the entire class is glaring at me now. Even with my lack of social experience, I know the kind of praise I just got--the kind given by a teacher at the expense of an alpha-- was the last nail in the coffin for my social status. I'm now doomed to be the girl with only one friend in this circle.

Professor Marsden elaborates, "Confirmation bias will haunt you at every stage of your life and there is no clear method to avoid its detrimental effects unless we learn to question our feelings and reactions at every turn."

I tune her out and bathe in my misery. I just blew my first opportunity to build a larger circle of friends, not to mention relationships. That's all I can think of right now.

The professor continues a speech that's like background noise to me, "Everything you are thinking this very moment, every opinion you have about something in your life, forms a preconception--a hard belief about that subject.

They will affect your life only if you allow them to sink in and influence your actions and decisions. Left to nature, then from this point forward, whenever you are reminded of these beliefs, you will cling to these beliefs and see only proof--even if nine out of ten real-life events say otherwise. The key is to understand this pattern, know when it is happening, and learn to detach yourself from these reactions."

Angela leans in to me and whispers straight into my ear, "You wanna go bait the local prey together after class?"

A new panic explodes into my mind.

I can't just say yes, I don't want to have to explain why I don't feed. I also can't say no... I'd feel like I'd be rejecting a potential friend and that's the last thing I can afford to do right now. I'm still shocked by how willing she is to make friends with me as it is. How can I pass that up?

I've decided. The social aspect has to take the front seat for now. I'll just come up with a way to avoid actually feeding in front of her.

I nod shakily. "Sure... Can we do something else though? I've done enough hunting for the week."

"It's okay, I know what you are, girl." She slaps my upper arm with a friendly grin.

"Umm, what?"

"Trust me. I know where to find some of the best flavor you've ever binged on. Seriously, you'll swear you're in vampire paradise when you taste one of these creatures."

"I don't know." I scramble for excuses. Mostly, I'm just confused by what she's implying. I don't think she has any idea what I do or don't do.

"Just come... for me?" She shoots me a trusting, friendly smile that no living vampire can say no to.

"Okay, okay. Fine."

She nudges me. "Good. I'll meet you in the clearing on the South-West end of the forest at four a.m."

After class, I stay behind to speak with Professor Marsden.

The Orange asks a long series of questions about when to hand in assignments, how to do it, what types of paper to use, and what color inks to use. I'm surprised she isn't asking how to walk.

I wait patiently.

I'm trying to be stealthy for now--to avoid any actions or sounds that might provoke further ridicule from that oddly-colored monster. I know she's just an idiot but she's like a queen, or one of the queens, ruling over this little circle.

I notice the boy, the one I was drawn to. He glances at me as he walks away.

My heart skips a beat. Was he really looking at me or was it something else? I look around like a paranoid maniac. Was there someone behind me? Next to me?

Nope, it really was me. Why would he look at me?

I imagine myself lunging at him, and then asking for his name, number, family history, occupation, and interests all within the snap of a finger... Of course, I don't.

Oh, no... Did he just look because he saw something ugly and repulsive? Maybe now he'll laugh about me to his friends.

All I can do is watch him walk away, like a human

vegetating in front of a softly glowing screen.

He's whispering to some short, skinny little red-head. Okay, he must be making fun of me now.

Every piece of my rationality says to me that I'm just being paranoid but I still can't help it. I think my brain just gets a few million times dumber and less rational when these things trigger my instincts. Cheers to primal mating instincts!

And then I overhear a bit of Orange's conversation with the professor.

"I understand the pressure." The professor leans in toward the citrus monster. "But it is always a choice. I have seen so many of my brightest and most promising students lost to Scarbromine addiction. It may be difficult to say no to her now, but you will not regret it five centuries from now."

Orange sighs and swings her arms down like she's flinging water off of them. "It's not like they're making me do it. We just do it, like, two days a week... It's a weekend thing, you know? It's just for fun."

"Scarbromine is a serious--"

"Yeah, yeah... So... you want the paper in at, like, five minutes after class starts, right?"

"That is correct. And do not avoid the subject. I am simply urging you to consider the consequences of your decisions. Please think about it."

Orange lets out a grunt from the depths of her throat. "Okay, see you tomorrow, professor," she switches to a high pitched tone as she walks away.

That creature finally gives me a chance to talk to Professor Marsden alone. The professor gestures to walk with her.

A bird flies overhead and fades into the cloak of

the smog in the sky. It looks a bit thinner than the smog in the city but still thick enough to cause a visibility hazard.

"I've been thinking," I begin, "do you think our species could ever take over the world? I mean, if we all form communities like this and all the humans are slowly dying off from the smog problems."

She smiles as if I'd open the door to a subject she already wanted to rant about.

"The human corporate leaders are panicked, scrambling to explain the causes, all the while developing new ways to expand their own power and wealth."

"So you think their greedy corporations caused it?"

"Not necessarily. The truth is never that simple. It is possible and probable that they are emitting the substance, but there is no conclusive data. We do not even know if the substance is a known pollutant or an entirely unknown chemical. To assume one way or the other would not be constructive to either species."

"So why'd you say all that about their leaders?"

With a reassuring hand on my shoulder, she continues, "Go back to the root of the problem, dear. The humans still live under old belief systems passed down through generations and generations. Even if these beliefs were once rooted in truth, they are so heavily distorted now...to the point where many of their people only follow the word of the law rather than the reasons and rationale behind those laws. What good is a rule if the people who follow it only follow it as a technicality with loopholes?"

"So you're saying people do things for the wrong

reasons? Don't we do the same thing?"

"Yes, we do. That is the problem."

"But isn't it kinda harmless? I mean, as long as we make the rules specific enough... It can still work for everyone, right?"

She shakes her head. "The problem, dear, is not the rules. The problem is the mindsets of the people who follow them. If our species is to become the new dominant species on the planet, it is our responsibility to teach our young generations to understand why it is counter-productive to violate the rules, to harm one another. Simply teaching them to follow the rules will produce the same kind of abuse of ethics we see from the human lawyers-- convictions and acquittals based on technicalities. It is the responsibility of the world's future leaders, who may or may not be of our species, to make the right decisions for the right reasons... not to find the easiest shortcut to hoard resources and wealth for oneself, or one's corporation, or even one's nation. We are simply not ready."

I pause and try to absorb it all. "But, I was asking if we could take advantage of the situation and become the new dominant species. I wasn't asking if we should."

She sighs from the bottom of her lungs. "And that, my child, is the reason we are not ready."

Professor Marsden and I continue to circle the forest and talk. She does most of the talking. Personally, I think she's just been aching to find a student that doesn't get bored by her ideas.

Most of the time, I feel like a newcomer--an alien to this community--but the professor and I both know all about what's happened to the humans in the past, one from books and the other from reality. At the least, we usually understand each other, even if we may not agree right away.

I guess being a crazy inner city loner finally helped someone else out somehow.

"So where am I gonna stay over-day when the sun comes up? Under a big tree?" I ask.

"Meet me before sunrise at my study area."

"And I'm supposed to know that is...?"

"It is in the Central Western section of the forest, a few minutes hunting-pace from where we came in. I will take you to an old community-funded apartment complex... It is managed by an old and trusted friend."

Before she turns to walk away, I ask, "Oh... just one more thing. What's Scarbromine?"

The professor screeches to a halt. "It is better that you are not aware of it, Iryna."

"How am I gonna know what I'm avoiding if I have no idea what it is?"

"I will give you something when you visit my lab. For now, please understand that it is a dangerous narcotic that is common for recreational use in our communities."

Quietly, I wait alone at the clearing on the South-West just like Angela told me to. After a series of yawns, I start wondering if I went to the wrong place.

Suddenly, I feel a kick directly to my hipbone that tremors through my entire frame.

It's Orange, Bleach and one other girl: that short, skinny little red-head that the boy was whispering to before. The way her eyebrows seem to be permanently raised, she looks about as smart as an air bubble so I'll name her Bubble in my mind for now.

It looks like Bleach delivered the kick. It's nothing worse than what I've dealt with in the city. I don't bother to even acknowledge them.

"What are you doing here all by yourself, new girl?" Bleach speaks up first.

I don't respond.

I just calmly sit against a tree and watch the clearing for my friend. And then it dawns on me, what if Angela was actually one of their ass-kissers? What if Angela told me to come here just to set this up? Maybe she's using me to advance her own social status in this clique.

"Answer her!" Orange commands as if I care.

Bleach pokes her finger into my mouth and tugs at my fang. "What's the matter, can't talk like you're all smart anymore?" She laughs at her own antics like she's out of breath. It's the most disgusting laugh I've ever heard.

I stare into the distance like nothing had even happened.

Orange pokes her finger lightly into my ear. "If you don't talk soon, you must be deaf, right? So I'll have to, like, open up your ears for you." Her finger moves deeper and deeper toward my eardrum.

Finally, I swipe at her artificially-colored face with the sharp tips of my fingernails.

She dodges it, somehow amused.

Bubble finally makes her contribution: She grabs my wrist, pins it against the tree, and whispers, "You know, I would've felt bad for you...but then you swing those dirty nails at my friend."

"You know these fake dolls aren't really your friends, right?" I reply. "Most people in the human cities are more mature than this by the end of high school. How old are you all anyway?"

"Ooh, she's calling us stupid again," Bleach calls out with her arms crossed. "Spread both her arms, girls. It's time to teach her some manners."

"This ain't the city, new girl. We don't live in garbage cans," Orange adds before she follows the order. I take another swipe at her but she manages to grab my other wrist and pin it to the tree--I'm forced to hug the tree trunk backwards. Maybe I underestimated them a little.

With my breast plate in the open, Bleach leans in and slices my shirt open by running her fingernail from my collarbone down... toward my heart.

"So..." Bleach smirks. "How long do you all think it'll take to get my claw through this flat little chest?"

"You honestly think I'd believe you're going to kill me here?" I look the platinum-haired bimbo in the eyes. "I've broken the arms of scarier-looking vampires in the city when I was fifteen."

Bleach winks. "Who said anything about killing? I just wondered how much pain you city girls could take before you'll bow down and lick between my toes." She aims the sharp tip of her fingernail directly at my heart. "See, I ain't that dumb, city bitch. I know a little about science. I know why it hurts us so much getting stabbed so close to the heart."

I burst out into a breathless laughter. "Yeah... I'm sure you're, like, a genius."

She doesn't quite go through with the stabbing.

Instead, she spends the next five minutes driving the hardest punches I've ever felt, directly at my heart. Surprisingly, with her tall lanky frame, she packs a powerful punch even by city standards-- but I would never admit it aloud. She doesn't deserve the pleasure of knowing.

I try my best to hide the pain, to keep her from getting the satisfaction--but I couldn't.

The pain is excruciating.

My head starts to feels light and empty. My body feels like it's falling down an endless pit. Hands and feet go numb. My eyes involuntarily light up.

The other two look shocked.

It doesn't look like they had expected this to really happen. My guess is the alpha bitch threatens to hurt people all the time, the kind of people she's afraid to be in the shoes of, and it always worked. It reinforced her social status. I just wouldn't fold and I must've pushed her ego over the edge by laughing right in her face. And now, I get to feel her pent up frustrations taken out within inches of my heart.

There's no way to break free. Bubble and Orange are stronger than they look, and it's two arms against each of my wrists. Bleach has an open target and I know she's not about to stop taking her frustrations out on me any time soon.

I calmly close my eyes and wait it out as I recall all the times I had experienced far worse in the city. Better yet, I'll lucid daydream a little...

CHAPTER 4

Adrian was born human, to a family that had been running small-time scams around the city since the day it was founded, originally as New Amsterdam, by the Dutch in 1625. Over the years, they always managed to get by...just under the radar.

The year was 1929 and Adrian was seventeen years old.

His father ran shady business the humans called a bucket shop. They were deceptive little operations where customers would come in and bet on stock prices, either up or down, with as little as a few dollars--or as much of their life savings as they were willing to gamble.

Now, I don't know much about those complicated human-made money games, but I was told these shops were illegal by then and Adrian's family was running one of the last surviving ones at the time.

On the real stock exchanges, no one would let you bet on the price of a few thousand shares with less than a hundred dollars but these bucket shops were more like gambling joints than stock exchanges. Most times, the shop would just pocket the customers' losses--and most of the customers would lose day in and day out--so Adrian's father was getting rich off their stupidity and gambling instincts.

At first, Adrian watched the stock prices on the boards together with the customers. Days became weeks...and then months...and eventually, Adrian noticed patterns in the crowd psychology.

He watched the faces of every customer and watched as prices moved up, stalled, and then reversed for a little, stalled again, and then continued upwards. The patterns got more and more obvious to him, yet not a single one of the customers seemed to catch on. Every time, they would buy at the top, panic, and then sell at the bottom, and panic again. Every day, his father got richer and the poor customers got poorer.

One Monday night in October 1929, Adrian had drawn up a chart and planned to show his parents when he was done. He found a pattern that could make them rich, he thought. He figured, if their family could play the game for real, they could stop scamming all these poor customers and just make money off of his observations.

"Dad, I've got something to show you," he told his father. But his father waved him away, occupied by a phone call. He grabbed his father's arm and whispered, "This is important."

His father impatiently smacked him across the face with a backhand.

Adrian didn't know what the phone call was about, but he felt utterly unappreciated that he would be treated like that after all the work he had put in to this project.

Adrian decided to get back at his father in the only way he knew how.

He knew--based on the patterns of crowd psychology he had seen over the past month--the market was going down on Tuesday morning. He didn't know by how much and he didn't care, all he knew was that it was going down first thing in the morning, even if it would be a small drop. His plan was to quietly inform all of the customers in the shop, first thing on Tuesday morning, to short sell the whole list.

Tuesday morning, Adrian watched the customers walk into the shop and, one by one, he approached them and told them that he had inside information on some of the biggest stocks in the country and it was a tip worth playing. "Sell, sell, and sell some more...and you'll make a killing today," he told them.

Well those customers just couldn't resist a good tip back then. Even if they didn't agree with Adrian's advice, a part of them thought maybe, just maybe, he was right.

In the human society's virtual money games, selling short just means you're betting that the price will go down--you sell short first and then buy it back later when it's lower--so the idea is to sell high, then buy low afterwards. In the bucket shop, the customers were basically betting against the shop that the price would go down.

If the customer bet one hundred dollars that the Union Pacific was going down by one cent, then the shop would owe the customer two hundred dollars if Union Pacific goes down two cents.

And so, the customers all sold short--thousands upon thousands of shares of everything the bucket shop had prices to. Even the ones who didn't follow Adrian's advice were simply too scared to buy, so no one was betting on prices going up. To encourage everyone to join in, Adrian himself made a five-hundred dollar bet at the front desk against his own father's business.

Adrian sure got his revenge that morning.

As it turns out, the customers in his father's shop weren't the only ones who didn't buy that morning-- the real market was doing the same thing and there was no end in sight to the selling. It was Tuesday, October 29, 1929--the day that would go down in history as Black Tuesday, one of the biggest stock market crashes in the history of this human nation.

Before noon, Adrian's father had to shut the shop down. They had lost every cent of their profits from the customers they had ripped off over the years.

In many ways, it was poetic justice...but Adrian had no intention of doing something so extreme to get back at his father. He thought, at the most, his call would be right for a few cents on each stock, and the shop would just lose a few hundred dollars for the morning--and then Adrian could show his father how it was all done.

But there was no one to show.

As it turned out, the people on the phone with Adrian's father were the Securities and Exchange Commission. The old man was making a deal to legitimize his business and merge with a new partner to become a proper, licensed stock brokerage, a full-fledged member of the exchange.

He had built up enough money over the years to make the shop legal and it was only a matter of days before the deal would have been sealed.

That night, Adrian wanted to give his father back his measly winnings...but he found his father's body, cold and pale on the kitchen floor with faded eyes. He never found out how he did it and he didn't ever want to know.

Adrian never forgave himself for that Tuesday morning. He took his blood money and brought it to a club in a rural upstate community he had heard about. He had no intention of letting himself live through the week anyway--he just wanted to experience a few new things before he died and a couple of his classmates told him it was the experience of their lifetimes.

He spent a small fraction of his winnings on a bus up to a rural part of Erie County. It was a scarcely populated area, compared to his home town. Across the water was a colorful strip at the edge of the Canadian human province of Ontario--a district designed by the locals to attract American human tourists to spend their U.S. paper money in the land of the moose and beaver. The club, however, was just on the shore of the American side.

As he walked down the front steps, he noticed a set of dark light tubes that were probably once fluorescent lights, smashed. Small pieces of glass were still strewn on the floor.

A woman dressed in a tight corset greeted him. He was ready to spend all of his winnings that night because he wasn't planning to stick around for much longer. His classmates had mentioned that he could buy the night of his life in this place. He thought he knew what that meant.

The lady escorted him to a backroom where two other girls, who looked to be around his age and pretty enough to be pin-ups in those days, reclined against a velvet couch. They stared at him with an intense focus and invited him to sit down, right between them. As a seventeen-year-old male, he didn't hesitate to oblige.

"What's your deepest, darkest wish?" One of the girls asked in a soft, seductive voice.

He answered casually, "I don't know about wishing, but I'm planning to die soon so I guess you could just go ahead and kill me while you're at it."

They both bared their fangs and their eyes glowed brightly in the dimly-lit room.

He looked them in the eyes and smiled with a sense of relief that they had also never seen before. He had no idea this was the kind of pleasure he would be getting but he was glad to find it.

The club had hired a bunch of high school students to spread the word about the place. The truth was none of Adrian's peers had even been to this end of the state.

Usually, the customer would ask for some over-the-top sexually deviant favor. The girls would surprise the customer with their own kind of treat. This time, the customer wanted death and didn't look the least bit surprised or fearful of their eyes or fangs.

The blonde on the right sank her fangs into Adrian's wrist. He winced for a moment but then closed his eyes and enjoyed it. He felt he deserved pain and suffering, and he was glad to receive it.

A minute later, the girl on the left bit down on his

other wrist and began to feed on him. Her fangs were a little smaller and not quite as sharp, so it actually hurt more when she bit down...but he didn't care anymore.

For the next five minutes, Adrian felt a natural high that he never thought possible. He felt empty and cold on the inside, and he didn't have one ounce of fear about it. He wanted it. He needed it.

Both of the girls slowly moved up his arm and worked toward his neck and then...

"Damn it!" The short-fanged one shrieked.

Adrian and the other girl both shot their eyes open and looked at the short-fanged girl.

A tall, brick house of a man storms into the room and asks in a voice with more bass than any speaker system in their day, "What happened? This one trying to fight back?"

"No, no." The short-fanged girl waved him away. "It's my fault... I bit my lip!"

Immediately, the big man took out a large battle axe and walked up to Adrian. He lifted it in the air and aimed it straight at Adrian's head...

"No!" The short-fanged girl shoved the big man with the force of an automobile. "I said, it was my fault. I really did bite my lip...you think I'd defend him if he did this? Just leave us."

The bodyguard promptly left the room and obeyed the girl's wishes.

Adrian had no idea what all this meant and he didn't much care. All he thought was that he was about to die, one way or another, so who the hell cares, right?

Adrian and the short-fanged girl stayed together at a cheap motel on the Canadian side of Niagara Falls that night. Back then, the border officials rarely even asked for I.D. if you declared yourself Canada and passports would not be required until more than eighty years later.

"What's your name?" Short-fangs asked gently with eyes that glistened from tears.

"Why's it matter?" Adrian replied with a smirk.

"Because you're going to be living with me for a very, very long time and the least I could do is ask your name."

Adrian had heard all kinds of stories about vampires. He never thought they really existed but he had known of a few different legends from the old books and black and white motion pictures of the time.

The turning of a human to a vampire had always been an event he imagined as a dramatic, and even romantic, moment where two beings connected and the human would be made into an immortal so that the couple could spend an eternity together. He imagined that it would be like a form of marriage where the moment would resonate deeper than any arbitrary human ceremony.

Well it wasn't very dramatic for him. He didn't even see it coming--and neither did the one who turned him.

It was just an accident.

For the next fifty-eight years, Adrian had long intended to end his own life--now his vampire life-- but he never went through with it. In fact, his maker stayed around and made sure he would never go through with it. Instead, his maker taught him the ways of the vampire species and helped him live among them. Eventually he began to identify as a member of the vampire species and came to view his former peers as nothing more than food.

Together, they helped to shape the history of Niagara Falls, Ontario, and eventually helped to plan and develop Clifton Hill--the area of bright, colorful, Las Vegas-like tourist attractions that signifies the Canadian side to this day. What began as human-owned bait for American human paper money became vampire-owned bait for blood from the red, white, and blue.

As far as Adrian was concerned, he had become pure vampire...until October of 1987, when he heard news of another major stock market crash suffered by the humans in his home town. It brought back all of the most painful memories of his past and reinvigorated his former identity as a human-born New Yorker.

To his surprise, his maker didn't argue much before she agreed to accompany him back to the city where he was born.

In the weeks following that fateful October 19th of 1987, Adrian roamed the Wall Street area for humans who gave off strong scents of depression. He had no idea how he was able to pick up these feelings, but it didn't matter to him--he simply knew what they meant. He figured it was a hunting instinct that could be turned to good use.

And so he tracked down every suicidal investor he could find and told each of them his own story from 1929. Since he still appeared to be roughly in his early twenties, he pretended that it was a story told from the perspective of his father who, he told them, was seventeen in 1929.

In the end, he saved twenty-two people who admitted that they were planning to commit suicide...and three others who denied they had ever planned to attempt it.

A little more than a decade later, following the collapse of over-priced technology companies, Adrian returned again to his home town. This time, he encountered a young girl, whose name he never learned, and whose existence he most likely forgot about within hours of meeting her.

That girl, of course, was me.

In Adrian's eyes, he had closed the book to his past in the city for the time being, and in the human species for that matter. For me, on the other hand, it was the beginning of years and years of attempted research before I tracked down an old, deceptive inner city storyteller who filled me in on her knowledge of Adrian's past.

The storyteller later betrayed me and she has since been known to me only as Leather Skin-- because of her thick brownish coat caused by an accidental exposure to direct sunlight. But none of that mattered to me. She gave me a clearer picture of the vampire who once shared my sympathy for our food source.

For now, Adrian is just an idealized dream to me. Maybe, one day, our paths will cross again. Until then, I can only dream.

CHAPTER 5

espite all efforts, tears begin to build up in my eyes. It's just a natural physical reaction--like pulling a nostril hair. It's definitely not emotional. The only emotion I feel is an overwhelming desire to rip the bleached-blonde alpha's head off but even that's probably not worth it here.

Bleach smiles with pleasure as she slows down and just rolls her knuckles, back and forth, over my already-bruised chest. She knows how much it hurts and she's making sure she gets the bang for her buck.

Behind her is a sight I'll probably never forget.

Angela appears over the horizon, running like a leopard. Her lips are tightly rolled up against the front of her fangs. "Hey!" She calls out as if the girls had been breaking into her property.

Immediately, the three bullies jump to their feet and run like they're being chased by a monster of mythical proportions. I'm a little torn between the joy of seeing my first, and only, friend prove her loyalty; and the disappointment at not having the chance to retaliate against Bleach at my first opportunity.

Angela chases them at full speed like a lion clearing its territory with fierce conviction.

I didn't think she'd have the social status to do this. I sure didn't think she looked intimidating enough for anyone to react to her like a rabid predator had been after them.

Well, the most important part is: she obviously didn't set me up after all... I realize how stupid I was for being suspicious of her now. Maybe I just need to stop being paranoid about everyone and adapt to a new environment.

Sure, three of the girls just proved that some people in this community aren't any better than the city females--maybe just a lot less mature--but I found my first true friend, apparently. It's probably worth getting used to.

After the three stooges disappear into the distance, Angela begins running back in my direction. She dashes toward me like a wild animal and lunges toward me with both arms extended. Normally, this would be the moment I'd get into a defensive position and be ready to throw her to the floor. But I can see that giant smile on her face, all warm and cuddly. I just want to hug her.

And I do.

We roll into a tight, warm embrace like long lost sisters meeting up for the first time in years. No one would ever guess we had only known each other for less than a day.

I still couldn't quite wrap my head around her kindness. I mean, why would an attractive vampire like her, a girl who apparently has some social clout around here, want to hang out with the outsider? Somehow, it all seems too good to be true but I guess I shouldn't look a gift prey in the mouth.

Maybe I should just accept it as my welcome into this strange new world of social vampires.

She stares at my slit-open shirt. In all the excitement of seeing her, I completely forgot to pull my shirt closed. I know exactly what she's thinking: she must be concerned about the giant bruise over my heart area.

"It's okay," I tell her with a smile as I pull my shirt over the damage like a half-robe. "It doesn't hurt as much as it looks like it does," I lie.

"That's a load of crap, girl." She gives my upper arm a friendly slap. "Don't let 'em treat you like that. Why didn't you, of all people, fight back? You could probably take their--"

"So I take it you fought back?"

"You could say that." She stares into my eyes for a moment and smiles.

"So, you said you knew where to find the best tasting prey on the coast?" As quickly as the words could come out of my mouth, I want nothing but to smack myself upside the head for picking the worst possible topic. Here I am, after stressing out about having to create an excuse to avoid feeding in front of her, and yet food is the first thing that comes to mind?

She grabs my hand. "Yeah. Come with me... You're never gonna regret this, girl. It's the best fresh prey a vampire ever could feed on. And not just in this region either."

She has the most mischievous little grin on her

face. I love it--maybe because it feels like a sign that I'm close enough to be trusted with secret exchanges of meaning.

"Hey, so how do you do it?" she asks.

"What?"

"Do you just dig in with your fingers or do you use some kind of scalpel or something? Don't worry... you can tell me. I used to do it too. I mean, I haven't had to lately but--"

"I really don't know what you're talking about."

She slaps my upper arm. "Hey, don't be keeping any secrets from me now, girl. Let someone in a little... Trust a little."

She looks at me for a moment, in silence. I honestly have no idea what she's implying and I'm not quite sure how to answer.

"It's okay, I get it. Let's just get a moving... you evil little thing." She slaps my upper arm again.

I'm beginning to think she looks for every excuse in the world just to slap my arm. I guess these semi-annoying quirks are the price of a real friendship.

She pulls out a clear bag from her pocket. It's a batch of cookies, of all things. "Time to catch us some gourmet flavored prey."

"Wait, what are the cookies for?"

"It's a special kind of bait for a very special kind of prey."

"Hey, you know anything about Scarbromine?"

She glares at me like I'd just insulted her mother.

For two hours, we quietly watch an open area of the forest like a couple of hungry hawks. Angela's cookies are sitting in the middle of the target area.

We crouch in a primal stalking position on all

fours, behind what's probably the worst smelling mound of dirt that's ever attacked my nasal passages.

Randomly, she glances at me with a loving smile so I smile back. It makes all the worries and risks and pain worth it--everything except for the smell.

"Can we just move over to the trees?" I ask with my nose scrunched up. "This stuff really stinks."

"No. We need it to drown out our scent."

"Since when do we need that? Humans have really badly underdeveloped senses, remember?"

"Quiet. You'll scare it away."

"Do you seriously think the cookies will work though? I mean, really, humans aren't *that* stupid."

"Shh!" Angela places a finger over my lips with a smile that's part loving and part annoyed.

And so we wait in silence--for half an hour.

I start night-dreaming a little. I look up and couldn't help but miss being able to see the clear, starry night sky with the moon shining down on us. I never thought any of us would see the day when the sky over a place like this would be as star-free as the inner city sky.

I drift off into my dream world.

Angela nudges me. "Snap out of it," she whispers. "Trust me. It'll all be worth it when you taste the flavor of these blubber bags. Stay awake and be patient."

And then Angela raises a hand in front of my face like some sort of organized hunting signal. I have no idea what she means.

I hear something.

I guess she was signaling that she'd already heard a sound. Maybe her practice is paying off. After all,

I haven't hunted in a year and a half.

The prey's feet crush the grass slowly, one step at a time...

It comes into view and it looks like it's walking into the target area--heading straight at the cookies. I couldn't believe my eyes.

There it is, in all its colorful glory: the prey falling for Angela's cookie bait. I wouldn't have believed it if I'd been told a million times but I can't deny the sight right in front of me. Have humans really gotten this stupid in this region?

Angela and I both get into a ready position. I arch my spine and focus on the target. My eyes illuminate.

The prey grabs the cookies. It seems to be uncontrollably drawn toward them. Why? There's no time to think.

Adrenaline fills my circulatory system. The fight or flight hormone has taken hold of me--and I'm not about to flee any time soon.

I can feel the natural high kicking in. I'm ready for the kill, my first kill in a little over eighteen months.

Angela makes the first move.

She leaps into the open and dashes toward the prey.

To my surprise, it seems entirely prepared for this attack. In fact, it almost dodges her. She slashes the side of its face with her sharp fingernails--but it catches her arm and throws her.

Her body flies through the air, but before she even lands on the grassy floor, I follow her lead and dash toward the prey with every bit of aggression left in me.

My long, sharp, primal fangs are fully exposed

even though I have no conscious intention of using them.

Thanks to the distraction from Angela's initial attack, I've got a clear path to the prey's throat, and I use it.

I launch my body into the air, soar toward the prey's head...

It turns around to face me.

It sees me for maybe a split-second. It reacts quicker than I've ever seen a human react.

It punches me... but it's not quite a punch. I think I've just been scratched!

There's no time to worry about my injury... I'm just shocked that a human can put up a fight like this--but this won't help its cause, it just brought the city hunter right back out of me.

I jump to my feet and take a quick swing at its neck. In one swift motion, I slash its carotid artery open with my razor-sharp fingernails.

Its eyes shoot open and freeze.

It's over.

But somehow, I can't stop. It's been so long since I've hunted like this. The adrenaline in my veins is pushing me at full force. Maybe it's because I've never felt like I was defending myself when I hunted before... it always felt more like a boring routine back then. This time, it feels like self-defense, maybe even a fight between peers. It feels personal.

As it drops to the ground, face first, I spring myself into the air, lift my knee... and drop my foot, with my entire body weight behind it, right onto its back.

Snap!

"Whoa! Easy there, girl." Angela pulls me off of the

prey. "I'm sure it's dead already, on account of what you just did to its throat!"

I feel my heart rate slowing down, gradually. My eyes finally relax.

Angela pats me on the back like a boxer's manager congratulating a newly crowned champion. I'm not sure I like it but I guess any kind of praise is better than ridicule.

"That was some beautiful hunting there though, I'll give you that." She slaps me on my upper arm with a smile. "You're turning out to be everything I expected. You want the first bite?"

Nervously, I shake my head.

I hope, with every inch of me that she doesn't ask again or insist out of some politeness ritual where she has to ask even though she knows the answer. I would like nothing more than if she would just dive in and finish it off. That way, I'd have no explaining to do.

She dives in and tears the prey's shoulder open; that gives me the relief I needed. She doesn't sip it neatly and gently like the hunters in the alley did, she mostly just rips it open like a little child that hasn't quite learned its manners yet. And here I was thinking people around here might have a more refined way of doing things.

But then... the real bomb drops.

Angela looks up at me, smiling with tendons and blood dangling and dripping from her mouth... She turns the body over, onto its back.

Suddenly, hiding my feeding disorder is the very least of my concerns. You might even say all of my problems, the ones I'd considered the worst things in the world only minutes ago, now seem like petty and childish footnotes.

The prey's mouth hangs wide open, with its entire set of teeth exposed.

It's a sight I'll never forget.

I can't believe I didn't see it the entire time. I blink, rub my eyes... and look again just to make sure I'm not seeing things. Unfortunately, I'm not.

My heart collapsed unto itself, like it stopped and fell straight to my stomach.

This can't be real, I think to myself, it can't possibly be.

I can barely feel my own lips moving, dried and numb, as I open them to mutter, "The prey. It's got fangs."

CHAPTER 6

hey say the professor just returned from her visit to the East Coast. I hear she brought some new girl back with her too but I'm too tired to care much right now. And I'm not the only one either. The whole crew is exhausted from our two week vacation, with all the partying and all of Courtney's excessive binging on our A.B. negative savings.

"Wake your lazy ass up, Adrian!" Courtney's voice screeches like a rusted train track.

It's nine o'clock at night...so it's time to wake up. With Courtney here, who needs an alarm clock?

Courtney is my heaven and my hell. I love her and I hate her, all at once...but you could say I owe her my life, and in some ways, I probably need her for my life in this community to continue.

It's time for our nightly routine again. Great.

Some people might think it'd be hot doing this with a girl like her, but it's nothing special anymore to be honest. Why would I expect it to be though? It started with nothing but an accident. What a way to start a life together that was.

I know she'll never like me the way I like her--in fact, she can't...because she could never get over what we can't ever do--but she's still doing me a huge favor every night so I couldn't ask for more. I don't deserve much more, now that I start thinking about it.

"Get over here, boy," she calls out to me like I'm her stray pet. "Let's get it over with, okay? Quick. Come on."

Ugh.

She's got that fake-looking orange colored artificial tan on again. She's been wearing that since we stayed in the Battery Park area. It's all well and good adapting to all the human cultural shifts and fashions and speech patterns, as best we all can over the years, but it comes with some annoying side effects. Maybe the elders would think I'm just as annoying carrying on the way I do.

Anyone who takes one look at Courtney today would be guessing she's still about eighteen to twenty years old, I'll give her that. It's the whole attitude thing maybe. I'm sure there's a lot about me that screams of some young human too, but I don't notice when I hit it on the mark, and when I miss by a mile, anymore.

Old habits die hard.

Three years into living in this community, and we both still act like we're living in Erie County, trying to blend in with present day humans in their degenerated culture. It's a different life out here, that's for sure. The biggest of those differences is I need to do this if I'm going to survive out here, even if it means swallowing some of that orange slop.

So, like a tired, old routine, she tilts her head over

and shows me that soft, smooth skin on her neck.

I close my eyes.

Suddenly, I have a craving for sweets! I need to control that damn craving. I don't know what it is but I get this insane craving for sugary foods, white bread, and all kinds of things like that--all the time. Courtney tells me she never gets them; I don't think any born-vampires can ever crave that crap. Maybe it's because I wasn't turned proper...or maybe all turned vampires have weird side effects, I wouldn't know. If there are any others like me around here, they're probably all disguising themselves as born-vampires the way I'm doing right about now.

Okay, focus. Focus, I tell myself.

I need to do this or they're all going to know what I am. Questions, they're the last thing I need right now. We've got class soon too.

Carefully, I sink my fangs into her neck.

The warm, metallic taste of her blood...it's dripping into my mouth like thick syrup. I wonder if they all taste like this or if she's just special. I doubt anyone else would let me try. Nothing we feed on ever tastes like this, that's for damn sure.

Even after all the times we've done it, it still feels like she's sharing her whole life with me. In fact, what's more important is that she's sharing her vampire signature scent with me for another day...but that sounds so cold and heartless of me to be thinking about right now.

I just like to think it tastes like nothing else I could ever imagine--just pure joy, freedom, and undying love that will last for--

"Okay, boy. That's enough," Courtney mumbles as she rolls her eyes.

Abruptly, she kills my thoughts and pulls away from me like I'm some repulsive, lower life form. She covers her neck, probably ashamed or humiliated by the whole thing.

That's okay.

Half the time, I'm just as ashamed that I need her as much as I do now. It's not the way it should be, for any of us. We're living a new life here and maybe, one day, I'll find someone else who can help me out with my scent problems.

For now, she's the best I've got and I shouldn't be complaining. She's helped me through so many years of self-destructive thoughts and she was even there for me when I needed to find redemption.

I doubt if any of it matters much to her though. If it does at all, she sure doesn't show it.

Either way, it's just another night, just another exchange, for both of us so I shouldn't be over thinking any of it... Even the first time wasn't romantic so why should these be? Courtney did her part, I tell myself. I don't expect anything else from her and she never expects anything else from me. There's no pressure this way.

Some of the men in today's human generation would probably remark, "She's hot! Even if you don't like her, just use her and move on." The ones who try, well, they're just going to be another one of her two-minute snacks and she's a lot more careful about bleeding on her prey ever since our fateful accident.

I'm always fighting everything I feel inside. I just have to keep telling myself, over and over again, I've got my vampire signature in my scent for another twenty four hours. That's all I care about right now.

It's just business.

Our first day back in class begins.

The Courtney, Jamie and Sara crew are laughing their little fangs off about some feeding accident at the party last weekend. Disgusting, that was, but they think it's funny.

The professor stands at the middle of the class and pauses. At first, I wonder if she just forgot her notes but...no. She just took notice of that new girl, and the little girl is sitting ten feet away from the rest of us.

At a casual glance, she's pretty enough. I'm trying my very best not to stare a moment longer, but I couldn't resist. Her scent seems oddly familiar but there's no way we could have met before. By that, I mean if I had met anyone who looked as attractive as she does to me now, I would surely recall her name. I don't.

"Come in to the circle and join us, Iryna," the professor says to the new girl.

So her name is Iryna. She's got a shot at getting in good with the crew if she plays her cards right today.

After a little back and forth with the professor, Iryna comes to sit in the circle, finally, and I get a better look at her. She's a little scrawny but there's something quietly alluring about this one and I still can't help but suspect that our paths may have crossed in the decades past.

The moment she opens her mouth, I know one thing about her: few, if any, of the other male vampires in this community would show a pinch of interest in her.

I find her attractive...but I assume it's the old

species in me taking control. It's that buried human part of me that just can't resist the old standards of beauty.

If I heard right, she grew up in my hometown. I can just picture, back home, she was probably one of the most popular girls with all those human males--she probably fed on them all the time because of that.

All I know is if she ends up being popular here, it definitely won't be for her looks. I don't think she really knows why yet either.

Of course, Courtney lucked out a long time ago in that department. She only got to be one of the most popular girls in this class because of her looks. It's definitely not her personality, that's only gotten more and more annoying and abrasive by the decade.

Right now, my eyes see nothing but Iryna. The way she looks down at the floor, so vulnerable and adorably timid.

Unfortunately, Angela is whispering to her and it seems they're destined to be friends, from the looks of it. That could be good or bad depending on how the girl handles it.

"Iryna. Do you have something to add to our discussion?" The Professor asks. She must have noticed Iryna's distraction.

For the next five minutes, Iryna rants on and on about confirmation bias. It's only her first day and seems to know more about this stuff than half the class does. She sounds intelligent enough.

And then Courtney takes notice as I struggle to keep my eyes off of the subtle contours of Iryna's thin but elegantly curved lips. Naturally, my maker decides to sling one of the least clever insults I'd ever heard come out of a vampire of her age. Of course, Jamie dives in for the double feature.

I figure Courtney and the crew will make a laughing stock of the girl for a week or two. But then it gets worse...

A few minutes later, I couldn't help but overhear Iryna whispering to her new friend, "Can I break her arms and teach her a lesson?" There's no telling how many of the others heard that little remark, but either she's so deaf that she has no idea how loud her whispering really was, or she's just looking for trouble.

In the corner of my eye, I see Jamie sharpening her already-razor-sharp nails against a rock. I don't bother to look over at Courtney again. I know exactly how she's reacting to this--it's the trigger she was looking for to beat the living daylights out of the poor little new girl.

After class, Courtney spends what feels to be an eternity, asking the professor any old question she could pull off the top of her little head. The entire time, Iryna stands there waiting patiently like she's got no place else to go. Courtney knows the poor girl is waiting. She's milking this for everything it's got. Little does she know, her questions are starting to make her sound like a brain-dead moron.

I can't stop looking at Iryna but she doesn't seem to notice or care. I'll bet she wouldn't even give me the time of night, if her senses are all working and she started nitpicking. There must be some subtle difference that sets me apart even if I don't know it. Oh, who am I trying to kid? Even if she was that observant, a girl like her, by city standards, wouldn't give me a second look.

"Hey, we better go," Sara whispers to me and pulls me along with her. I think she noticed me staring and doesn't want me to get in trouble with the other two. Sara might be the only one with a conscience left after everything that's happened. I just wish she'd stand up for herself a little more.

And then I overhear the professor starting the old Scarbromine lecture again, that clever old woman. She sure knows how to shut Courtney up and fast.

"So what were you thinking about when you were looking at her?" Sara whispers with those innocent little raised eye brows of hers.

"Umm, nothing. Really."

"Don't lie to me, stupid head," she shoots me an adorable, childish little grin.

I lean in and whisper even quieter, "Well could you guys just take it easy on her? I know how Courtney and Jamie are, but I just--"

She stops and puts a hand on my shoulder. "I'll try...but you know how it works."

Adrian Thornton

CHAPTER 7

he very sight of a fellow vampire's corpse, frozen with its eyes in suspended shock, is a chilling sight all by itself. But never before has it meant what it does right here, right now.

"What's wrong, girl?" Angela asks, oddly casual in her tone. "Iryna..."

I don't answer but it's not really a choice--I can't right now.

It's one thing to talk tough back in the human jungle, where every female vampire threatened to rip another one's head off. It's another to actually go through with it. I've broken a few of my rival's arms; snapped a few ankles; and even scarred a few backs when I was fifteen and crazy on hunting addiction...but I never killed my own kind on purpose. This one was on purpose--even overkill.

Even more so than anywhere else, here in a strong community, the killing of one's own species is a taboo that no civilized being would touch--especially if it's for your friend to feed on.

On the way here, Professor Marsden mentioned

that the process of settling legal disputes is still a bit sketchy right now. There are no elected judges or juries or even official laws drawn up yet. People have tried, but no one could agree on anything-- everyone has their own agenda and people like the professor, who legitimately want morality and ethics to prevail, have little to no power in the grand scheme of things.

For now, the most common process is for the regional leader to decide the method of trial and the method of punishment. I haven't seen anything like that yet but I know the punishment for this won't be anything merciful.

If someone asked me even an hour ago what I would do in a situation like this, I would probably say I'd go mute for days or years...or maybe even flee the community to avoid all social contact with fellow vampires.

But right here, in the reality of it all, my reaction is much less predictable even to myself.

Sniff... Sniff...

Repeatedly, I sniff the body of the prey--over and over again--and somehow try to explain to myself how or when I went wrong. What's wrong with its scent? Why can't I smell the vampire signature in it? Was I blinded by something?

"Damn it! What's wrong with it?" I ask rhetorically, mostly to myself. "What's wrong with it? What's wrong with it?!"

Angela gently places a hand on my shoulder.

I kneel over the murdered vampire and wonder, how could I be so stupid? How could I not recognize the scent of a fellow member of my own species? There's no excuse. How could I not notice the most obvious signs--the fangs and the eyes--when it defended itself? How could I be so self-absorbed in the moment that I didn't even notice?

The fact is none of those questions even matter anymore.

Looking at the face of the corpse, the finality of its death sinks in. The shock in its eyes feels like a reflection of my own emotions right now.

I look up at Angela like a curious pre-school student who just used a red paint brush for the very first time. I want to ask her how she could possibly not know it was a vampire...but no words come out of my mouth. I just look at her in silence. Immediately, I push those thoughts out of my head. *That's just ridiculous*, I think to myself. *She couldn't possibly have knowingly done this. Somehow, I already know she wouldn't do a thing like that.*

She gives me a supportive smile and runs her hand down my back softly. "It's okay, girl. I won't tell anyone. I already know it's not your first time. Just sling it over your shoulder and follow me."

"Wait, you mean you knew all along? You knew?"

She lowers her voice and smiles, "I wasn't all that sure before but now that I've seen it with my own eyes, I know what you are. You're amazing at it. Just trust me--I'll handle it from here on out. We're in this together, Iryna."

I'm still not sure what she's getting at but none of it matters now. There's no time to think or ask questions; either I follow her lead and get through this together or I stay here and let the entire community crucify me for killing a fellow vampire. Even in my state of mind, it's not a hard choice. There's plenty of time to feel guilt and figure out answers later.

I promptly toss the body over my shoulder and follow Angela. She seems to know what she's doing and I know she genuinely wants to help me.

Along the way, I couldn't help but notice that I have no idea if the body is a male or female of the species. It also has a strangely ambiguous scent. Maybe it's not a real human or a real vampire--I'll tell myself that for now. It'll make it easier to carry the load on my shoulder.

Angela leads me deep into the forest. We stop at a giant cabin that looks to be made mostly of damp, muddy wood surrounded by hoards of insects. Chunks of mud and leaves stick to its walls and rooftop. It's not the most impressive thing a city girl could ever see--at least judging by the outside.

Inside, stark stone walls frame a single, sturdily-built, room. It looks like the entire cabin had been hollowed out and its guts were transformed into a stone box. The entire cabin seems to be empty except for a fireplace and a stairwell in one corner.

"This way," Angela mumbles as she leads me toward the stairwell.

"What is this place?" I ask as we spiral down a number of underground floors.

Angela chuckles. "Oh, I forgot. They don't have places like this in the city, do they? You'll see."

Between my awe and the side of the corpse scraping against my face, I lose track of how many floors there are in total. All I know is that we finally stop at the very bottom of the spiraling stairwell before we enter a cold, metallic hallway.

It feels like a style of building that's vaguely derived from ancient human architecture, but somewhere along the way, it branched out into a whole other direction. While the humans ended up with the blocky stone columns I was familiar with in the city, the vampire communities advanced into these underground castles--modernized in its own unique way.

I would imagine different tribes and regions would have developed different branches of these designs.

We enter a stone-walled hallway, lit by tall glass-encased candles. Only the tops are open, every side looks a little burnt from the heat of the flames.

"This is where I live," Angela announces proudly.

"You mean this whole place is yours? You must be rich..."

"No, dumbass. My apartment's down the hall."

I scramble for the first distraction. "Well those candles on the wall are cool. That's some energy-efficient lighting right there."

She laughs at me. "They're fake, city girl. This is the Ruthven Apartments complex, not some budget place. Those candles are powered by Niklaus Ruthven's private power generator...like everything else that's underground in this area." She burst my romantic bubble about some super environmental version of civilization.

I guess both species progressed along the same lines, just with different styles.

We turn a corner and pass tens of solid-looking metal doors.

"This corpse is getting heavy," I complain.

She finally stops at a door and whispers, "We're here. And, umm, let's not go calling it that in the hallways, huh?"

Angela's finger is illuminated by the green glow of

an electronic keypad. After a few clicks and beeps, and the sound of a hammer against hollow metal, the vault-like apartment door opens with a smooth swish of air.

Before I follow her inside, I notice a set of large double doors at the end of the hallway, glossy crimson with a cheesy frame. It strikes me as tacky and pretentious but I'll bet that's where this Ruthven landlord stays--either that or it's a penthouse with a heart-shaped bed, shades of the boroughs.

Angela's unit is a nice little white-walled studio apartment. The walls are mostly covered in charcoal figure drawings, and what little of it isn't covered has random scribbles that I'm sure the landlord would appreciate.

She seems to have a female-only policy with her figure drawings. Maybe she only feels comfortable drawing female models--what a sweet and innocent little girl she still is behind that tough exterior.

Still carrying the corpse, I browse through her kitchen and bathroom out of curiosity. It's not exactly an uptown penthouse but it's cleaner and more spacious than anything in a student's price range back in the city.

"Just drop it over there by the fridge," she points to an expensive-looking, stainless steel, double-the-size-of-a-casket refrigerator.

I literally drop the dead vampire.

Smack!

Its head hits the fridge door with the sickening sound of mushy flesh compressed between an appliance and a skull.

"Sorry," I mutter softly as I adjust the head.

Angela smiles at my reaction. "I'm pretty sure it's not gonna be mad at you for that, girl." She paddles through stacks of clothing in her drawers.

I notice a series of louvers across the top of the wall, above her bed. Curiously, I poke at it. "What are these for?"

"Air ducts, miss observant. At least two of us in here are still breathing, remember?"

"But where do they go?"

She laughs. "What, you planning to pull a Hollywood in here? I've seen that human crap too. Believe me, not even your little ass can fit in those things."

"No, I mean where do they come out?"

"Oh, I don't know. It's not like I built the damn place."

She pulls out a series of tops, and one after another, she compares the size of it against my body. And one after another, she shoves them back into her drawer and shuffles through for the next candidate.

I move in for a better look. "Want me to help? What are you looking for?"

"Something for you to wear. Ugh-- Something's gotta be small enough."

"Why? For what?"

She points at the side of my torso with her eyebrows scrunched like I had just asked the dumbest question on the planet. "'Cause you look like you just killed someone, you darned fool. Why'd you think?"

I finally look down and see a deep crimson pool spreading from my rib cage. I poke it. It seems to sting worse now than when the corpse caused it.

She's right. It's obviously not the kind of wound that a fit, teenage or adult vampire would get from routine hunting. It's a dead giveaway that either I killed another vampire or I got into a brutal fight with someone. Either way, people are going to start asking questions--and we both know that's the last thing I need right now.

She tosses me a small tank top. "Here, try this one on. It should do for now."

I stretch my arms overhead and begin to slide it on.

Suddenly, I can feel her staring at my body.

Her eyes are partly shut, like she feels bad for me maybe. Or maybe she's just afraid I've got other wounds that I haven't noticed yet.

Right before I pull the top over my wound, she grabs my hand and tells me, "Wait... let me soak it up first."

With a clean white towel from another drawer, she slowly, gently, soaks up the blood--gathering the fresh bits and some of the dried crusted pieces. I don't feel the sting of the pain anymore but she traces the contours of my ribs so carefully, so meticulously, I'm starting to think she's afraid to hurt me.

"You don't have to be that gentle." I smirk.

She smiles with a sparkle in her eye. "You're a strong little hunter. I like that."

"Why'd you say that?"

"You just are. You're a smart, beautiful, strong woman. I bet if you really tried, you could kick those three bullies' asses to the moon, girl."

The towel's pretty much turned into a soaking red ball.

I catch her eyes again, meaning to thank her for being such an amazing friend, but the words don't come out. I just stare, amazed that she thinks so highly of me for some unknown reason.

I think she gets it though. She smiles back at me with a look of shared meaning.

Come to think of it, I would never be this kind to anyone who just moved into my hometown, even if it had been the other way around. It gives me a deep sense of guilt admitting this to myself, but I know it's true. She's a better friend to me than I ever would've been to her.

The blood-soaked towel drops to the floor...and she drops to her knees.

"What are you doing?" I ask.

She brings her face closer and closer to my wound and replies with a mischievous smile, "I'm finishing up."

Gently, she picks up the remaining drops of blood with her tongue, tracing the ridges of my rib cage. Her saliva feels warm and surprisingly soothing. It actually feels good--and I didn't think it would.

How did she know to do that? I think to myself.

It doesn't even need to be said that I never would have gone to these lengths to help a newcomer. She truly is a better friend than I'd have been to her.

Finally, she finishes up. There isn't a single trace left of the wound except for the thin lines of the original slashes.

"Done and done." She winks with a satisfied smile.

For the next half hour, I try my very best to tune out the sounds of her breaking apart the dead vampire's carcass. Piece by piece, she packs the dead vampire away in her fridge. Her expertise at it is more than a little disturbing. I figure it's because she keeps a lot of leftovers on a regular basis so it's become second nature to her.

It's just not something most of us would like to see or hear being done to the body of a member of our own species. With any other ones, we can rationalize with scientific testing, population control, or separating parts as consumer products-- but for our own kind, it's the ultimate vomit inducer.

I run for the door faster than she probably expects me to, "Okay, it's been fun. I'll see you in class tomorrow."

Outside, I lean against the nearest tree by the cabin and puke more than I have in my entire remembered life.

"You okay?" A male voice asks. It's him, the dark-haired boy from my class--the one I was strangely drawn to since day one.

I scramble to wipe up all the bits of gooey, chunky, regurgitated red substances from my mouth and try to look as pretty as I can. Meanwhile, I'm feeling a little light-headed and I shouldn't be surprised either--I probably just lost most of my last lunch...from a year and a half ago.

"Here, have some of mine." He offers his arm with a gentle smile.

"I...can't." Awkwardly, I turn to walk away before I fumble my words like the idiot I am in these situations.

He looks unexpectedly disappointed but I think it's just good acting on his part. Chances are he just felt guilty seeing the little new girl puking her guts out by a tree--it's just a matter of politeness to offer some help. He probably would've hated me if I was rude enough to accept it.

Besides, he probably finds me repulsive.

CHAPTER 8

After meeting up with Professor Marsden at her study area, she leads me through a seemingly endless path to my new home. It's been a long night and my legs are beginning to feel limp and rubbery.

She pats me on the shoulder. "Do not be alarmed when you see it for the first time, dear. The community-funded apartment is a temporary arrangement but it will do for the time being."

As I follow her into a cabin, I realize that the exterior is the only part remotely comparable to Angela's complex.

In the main underground hallway--which is a little more accurately a giant wormhole--the chunks of mud, sticks, and nails that qualify as walls are lit by sagging coal mine-style lamps. I'm surprised there's even electricity in this place, to be honest.

We turn a corner and enter an oh-so-luxurious unit composed of two-by-fours, squishy brown substances that I hope is entirely mud, and a few stones here and there for added wall support. There's a small double-size mattress in the corner, with a clean white bed sheet over it that's thin enough to reveal the prominent stains beneath.

Well, at least the pillow looks nice and fluffy. Who am I kidding? The entire place reeks of mold and horse radish.

"This is your new home," the professor tells me. "Please excuse the odor. There are many addicts in this complex and the bylaws are difficult to enforce under the current political climate."

I try to force a smile and thank her, but I couldn't quite manage it while my nasal passages are being assaulted beyond belief.

Finally, I remind myself of the standards of living in the city if I had been as broke as I am now, and I finally respond, "Thank you... It's very nice."

"No. It is a veritable hell hole," the professor exclaims. "Pardon my French...but it is the best you will find in this region--until you become a functioning member of our community's work force."

My breathing is now done entirely through my mouth as I force a little grin.

Behind me, a man enters the room.

He looks to be about five feet tall with an eye patch over his right eye and lips that are oddly thick and rippled--only partly covered by a thick, furry beard.

When I first look directly at him, I flinch.

I quickly try to hide my reaction, and pretend I was just stretching, but it's too late.

"Iryna, meet Donat," the professor introduces the man. "This facility was once his residence before he moved on to bigger and better things. Today, he lives in one of the world's most luxurious vampire apartment complexes... but he continues to manage this old community-funded complex as an act of charity for the less fortunate."

"I am very pleased to meet you, Iryna," the man says in a hoarse and raspy voice. He kisses the back of my hand. "You are an exquisitely beautiful young woman."

"uhh-- thanks?" I reply with an awkward, nervous smile and a misplaced inflection. "So your name is...*Donut?*"

"It is Do*nat*...Dee, Oh, En, Aye, Tee...Donat. It is a name of Slavic origins, meaning given."

"Thank you for 'given' me a place to stay then." I immediately cringe at my own words.

"Do not be so nervous, dear," the professor interrupts my stupidity, "he is an old and trusted friend."

Donat adds, "If you require any assistance in this residence... Any at all... I will attend to it right away."

I nod with an odd little forced smile.

Looks like I'll be visiting Angela's apartment most of the time until I find work in this community.

As soon as the professor and Donat leave me alone, I fall dead asleep on the mattress in my new germ infested apartment.

ARIES BRAEBURN

The world fades away from me.

I wake in a small bedroom that feels distinctly familiar. A wind chime casts a long shadow across the entire room.

It's dark out. We need to get up soon...if we haven't already overslept.

I look down at my body. I'm about eight to ten years old, at the very most but I don't remember this moment. Maybe it's just a hallucination--as vivid as it is...I'm probably just dreaming this up. I must be.

Another little girl tugs at my arm. Her cold, baby blue eyes glow and stare at me like a statue that had come to life.

She looks just like me, except for the color of her eyes...and she's about the same age too. Meaning, she's about eight to ten years old right now.

"I hear something," she whispers to me in a chilling calm voice--strangely calm under the circumstances, especially.

"What is it?"

"Relax, Iryna." She reaches toward me quickly and adds, "I'm giving you something to relax."

I never got a good look at what she had in her hand, but I feel a sharp pain in my neck.

I pick up the distinct scent of horse radish.

My arms and legs begin to feel tingly and hollow...and my eyes feel heavier and heavier.

Blue eyed girl runs out of the room and shuts the door behind her. I want to reach for her and tell her to come back, to keep me company...but I can't seem to move my mouth. I want her to be here with me. Somehow, I know and feel that I love her.

An adult male's voice cries out and practically tears through the walls of the entire house. It seems to echo within the hollows of the wall behind me. I've never heard a man cry for help with such terror and desperation but it feels so familiar at the moment that my spine feels as cold as ice.

Not a minute later, a grown woman's voice rings out at the same volume--but with a much, much sharper pitch. Even through the muffle of the walls, I can hear the utter surprise and panic in her throat.

More than ever, I want to cry out for help, for the girl to come back and be with me, to not be alone in here...but I can't. I'm frozen in place, conscious but tingling with eye lids heavier and heavier.

The screams die down.

Minutes upon minutes pass and the scent of horse radish seems to die down...and then I can finally move again.

I slowly stand up off the bed and pull a deep breath into my lungs until it pushes my chest outward. I step onto the carpeted floors, one foot at a time, and feel my toes crush the fibers of the carpet with every step I take. The floor boards creak as the pressure of my body weight moves along the length of the room toward the bedroom door.

The doorknob feels cold.

After another deep breath, I turn it...and slowly step into the dark hallway.

I turn right.

The blue-eyed girl stands alone and stares at me, seemingly frozen in place, with her sky blue eyes and smiles. Thick red chunks drip from the pale skin of her bare little hands.

I feel a chill down my spine...yet I know I should love her--and I still do. I want her to be safe.

"What happened?" I ask and inspect her gore-

drenched hands.

"It was a bad man with a gun, Iryna," she whispers with a flat calm.

"An armed robber? Like a human one, right?"

She doesn't quite nod. She just smiles. "I killed it. We're safe now."

I walk toward the large door at the end of the hallway. A pool of thick, crimson liquid slowly spreads across the floor like spilt food.

My head feels cold as I wake. Beads of sweat are dripping down my face. My heart is pounding.

Was I just dreaming with my sick, twisted imagination? Or was it a real memory?

I don't know...but apparently, I'm outside now. I'm not in the apartment anymore. How did I get here?

CHAPTER 9

It looks like I've been sleepwalking through the forest in broad daylight--how I avoided the direct sunlight, I have no idea. I mean, I'm still alive right now so it's safe to assume I did. Maybe my subconscious was recklessly trying to avoid the foul odors in my new home.

I find myself in the middle of...something I've never seen before.

Entire families of vampires--old and young alike--are outside during daylight hours, covered only by the shade of the trees. It's pretty much our kind's equivalent to a large gathering of humans outside past midnight, except these people are probably risking their lives a bit more.

They've set up a giant cluster of display booths, showing off everything from charcoal drawings and oil paintings to strange objects that I would guess are original inventions of theirs.

The drumbeats of live music ring through the forest, over-shadowed only by the constant ambience of local vampire chatter.

I've never seen this area of the community before, let alone anything like it in the entire world. I must've wandered pretty far from the apartment. Judging by the position of the sunlight through the trees, I'm guessing this is the North East corner of the forest.

"Hey! Little pretty girl!" A short rotund man waves to me. His booth consists of a stack of what look to be large, clear bottles. "You cannot go wrong with these glasses," he tells me in a choppy accent with almost no vowel stresses.

In a closer inspection, the bottles are made of two layers of glass with some sort of clear liquid permanently trapped in between.

Reaching down behind the booth's front desk, he unscrews the lid to another glass that looks similar. He pulls something thick, solid, and red out of it...

Flop!

He slams a slice of raw meat on the table and lifts one end of it. He milks clear red liquid from it into the glass. "Here...try. It has been stored in the same type of cup for more than two days."

"Oh...umm, no...but thanks. I already fed." I start backing away as if he'd offered me some cheesy flyer in the city.

"Please. Try. You are skin and bones." He smiles invitingly as if that would be a bad thing if it were true.

Returning an awkwardly forced smile, I slowly take the glass and drink from it. Only, I don't really drink it--I roll it under my tongue and drool most of it out.

A man in a suit passes by and stares at me like I had never learned my table manners.

I put the glass back down. "You're right, it really is good...so what's it do?"

"It is called Fresh Feed Glass. Keeps blood warm, at ninety-eight point six degrees, for up to seventy two hours."

"Wow. That's a pretty cool idea...good luck with it."

"Very good for travel, little girl. You are from Los Angeles, no?"

"No, actually, I'm from--"

"What is your native blood type?"

"My what?" I slowly distance myself.

"Native blood type. Your genetic blood type-- meaning not that of your prey, but your own."

"Umm, I don't really know. But I can't afford to give any right now, I--" Suddenly, it dawns on me that I just contradicted my claim that I had already fed today. In a sudden panic, I run away from the booth, turn a corner through a series of painters' booths, and stop at a series of charcoal drawings.

I slow down, turn to look behind me, and try to catch my breath. I'm just hoping I didn't look too suspicious running from a vendor like that. Maybe some security guy is going to think I stole something.

"Hey," a tall, lanky girl in a sleeveless shirt taps on my shoulder, "what do you think of these?"

I turn around and see a large collection of figure drawings. The elegant figures of female vampires in various stopped-in-action poses are depicted in beautiful waves of simple lines. They look familiar.

She leans in closer. "I'm just getting rid of these because my ex left them in my apartment and I don't want anything to do with her anymore."

"Her?" I ask and try not to sound disapproving or

shocked in any way--just in case.

"Yeah, her. Say whatever you want but I'm proud of it."

"I didn't mean to--"

"The point is...I'm getting rid of these things as soon as I can, and you look like a nice girl so I'll give you ten for a teaspoon."

"A teaspoon of...?"

"What do you think? Or a quarter teaspoon of some A.B. negative if that's what you got native."

For a moment, I just stare into her eyes. She looks like someone's hurt her before and I'd actually feel a little guilty for saying no.

I move closer and tilt my head. "Take as much as you like," I whisper.

Her eyes widen in pure shock like a human street vendor who had just been handed a thousand dollar bill.

Quietly, she moves in and gently wraps her arms around my waist. I feel the tips of her subtle fangs as they press into the side of my neck. Deeper and deeper they sink until...with a little pinch, my skin breaks.

Holding thirty--that's right, thirty--drawings, all rolled up under my arm, I head back toward my personal realm of foul odors.

I figure I'll need sleep for class tonight so I can't stay up all day.

On the way back, I run into Bleach--literally. The drawings scatter all over the floor and I immediately expect a huge barrage of not-so-clever remarks out of her mouth.

In a silent panic, I gather up all the drawings and roll them back up under my arm.

To my surprise, she doesn't say a single word about it. She doesn't even laugh or have to hold back any laughter. She just holds her hands up, not quite over her head but more just in front of me, like I'd shoot her if she didn't.

"Hey... I'm sorry about what happened before. Let's just be friends, okay?" She says softly.

I don't bother to make eye contact. "Whatever. I'm going back to sleep now. You probably should too."

"It's Iryna, right? My name is--"

"I really don't care what your name is, okay? Bye."

She stands alone and watches as I walk away. I didn't care what her name was before and I still don't after she tortured me with her knuckles. As far as I'm concerned, her name is Bleach.

I enter the muddy hallways of the community apartment complex and pick up a distinct scent-- well, other than mold and horse radish, I mean. It's a fellow vampire.

It's Angela.

She stands waiting in the middle of my apartment, squeezing her nostrils together and breathing through her mouth. "I've been looking all over for you for like half an hour, girl. Where've you been?" She sounds like a human with a cold. "I heard where they put you and it ain't right." She furiously grabs my arm and pulls me along with her.

The charcoal drawings scatter all over the floor.

"Where'd you get those?" she asks with undeniable shock in her eyes.

"Umm...some girl at that market thing in the North East."

She pulls me even harder and forces me to follow her, leaving the drawings behind.

ARIES BRAEBURN

I try to slow her down, to no avail. "What's the hurry?"

"I'm hurrying 'cause I gotta get your little ass a job...so you don't have to live in this dump. Nobody deserves this."

She drags me through the forest, back to the Ruthven Apartments complex. Only this time, she doesn't stop at her own apartment--she leads me straight to the big, cheesy, double doors at the end of the hall.

"What's in here?" I finally ask.

"We're gonna see the boss, girl. Weren't you paying attention?"

"Your boss lives here?"

"He's not just my boss. He's the boss. He's the man...the one who owns all this."

This must be the landlord of landlords to command that kind of respect from a tenant and employee. I never even asked what Angela does for a living--I always figured she was a student holding some United Tribes equivalent of a part-time retail job. Maybe she cleans apartments--I'll ask later.

Angela knocks on the door. "It's me, sir."

I hear a beep and the sound of a hammer on metal. The doors swoosh open.

Suddenly, I'm even more amazed at the high tech features of this complex, after the place I'd taken a nap in...Oh no, I hope I don't smell!

"Come on in," a man's deep, booming voice echoes through the apartment.

It feels like a whole new world. My thoughts of the future are brought to a halt as the entire interior reminds me more of the past.

Deep crimson walls converge into a golden

Victorian era fireplace. A large office chair faces away from us, behind a wooden desk that appears as thick and solid as a miniature brick house.

"Sir," Angela addresses the back of the chair, "I brought Iryna Balmont here to see you."

"Balmont... Balmont..." the man replies, "oh...the Blonde Butcher?"

"That's the one," Angela confirms with a proud smile.

Wait...the Blonde Butcher? How or why did I get that label? Did Angela tell him about the body? No, she couldn't have--she'd be as guilty as I would be.

Oh well, I shrug it off, there's no point being confrontational with my new best friend's landlord. Maybe they've just got a sick sense of humor.

The man turns his chair and stands to offer his free hand--and by free, I mean the hand that isn't holding a glass of wine and a cigar like they're vital appendages.

My first reaction is that his crimson robe must have been carefully chosen to match the furniture and walls of the apartment--in both style and period.

A pretentiously comforting you-can-trust-me smile on the man's face is flanked by thick Mutton chops, and dark locks tied back into a pony tail.

"I am Niklaus Ruthven," he introduces himself with crisp clear annunciation, "I welcome you to my domain, Miss Balmont... a domain that some would call the greatest structural achievement in the history of the species--but I prefer to remain humble in spite of my accomplishments."

He shakes my hand with a firm grip.

My first impression of Ruthven is that he's just

another wealthy land owner--one who likes to boast under a very thin veil of humility, at that.

I notice he doesn't quite smell like a vampire though. Am I losing my sense of smell lately? Why do so many vampires not quite have the vampire signature around here? Maybe it's a rural thing, I'm beginning to think.

On top of everything else, I wonder how and why a simple property owner, albeit a very nice property, would imply that his complex is the greatest structural achievement in the history of our species. There must be other places like this somewhere. I'm sure he's not the only wealthy vampire in the United Tribes or other communities around the world. In all honesty, it strikes me as incredibly arrogant at first.

"Would you like a beverage of any kind?" Ruthven asks. "Or perhaps a batch of leftovers?"

"No, thanks," I reply.

"Oh, I apologize. I should know better. I have heard that you do not feed on your prey." He turns to Angela and laughs with shoulders pumping up and down. "This one only targets a man's heart."

I don't get it.

Did he somehow find out about my feeding disorder and decided to ridicule it so bluntly and distastefully? Does everyone tell their landlords everything around here? Something about all this doesn't smell right but I'm in no position to say anything just yet.

He turns to me again and continues, "You know, Miss Balmont... you are a lucky girl. I have known Angela for many years and I am confident that she will take great care of you. You will be very happy together."

He sits back on his throne.

I glance at Angela for a second.

She returns my glance with a warm smile that practically wraps my heart with affection. I guess she's made a lot of people feel this way. In all honesty, she may not be the smartest vampire I've ever met, but she seems to be a genuinely caring and loving person--with a stamp of approval from her landlord, as it turns out.

"I agree," I respond to Ruthven, "she's a very kind and caring vampire."

Ruthven gestures toward two small chairs directly across from his desk. "Go ahead. Take a seat."

On the mildly uncomfortable seat, I finally start to feel a bit more like I'm here for a job interview.

"I understand this is your first time in this region?" Ruthven asks while he lights his cigar.

"Yeah, it is," I reply.

"How do you like it here so far?"

"Well, I grew up in the city and, umm, I've only ever hunted in a city before, so...this is all very strange and new to me. Being around a whole friendly tribe of vampires, I mean. But yeah, I like it. It's new in a good way." I stumble over every word. Maybe it doesn't sound as bad to him as it does in my own head, but I feel like I'm screwing up my first impressions with Angela's landlord.

"Indeed, Miss Balmont... Now, I take it you are aware of my position in this area?"

"Yeah, of course. You're the owner of this underground apartment complex, right? It's a very, very impressive structure, sir." I smile and try to hold back before my nose is completely brown.

"And...?"

I fall dead silent. Am I forgetting something? I don't know. I just stare at him, confused.

A shock of ego injury overcomes the man's face. Did I over-do it and make him feel pathetic? Or maybe I said something wrong. I'm trying to remember every word I just said, just in case, but--

I glance at Angela for a little non-verbal input. She just glares at me like I'd insulted the president of a nation or something. I have no idea what I said wrong though. Are they not called apartments anymore? Did I use an offensive term? Should I have phrased it more carefully?

Flustered, I ask, "I... I'm sorry. Did I say something wrong?"

Ruthven adjusts the collar on his robe, as if to wipe off some offensive substance that'd just been thrown at him.

He clears his throat. "I am Sir Niklaus Ruthven, the man responsible for uniting ten of the twenty-one most powerful tribes in the West Coast. Once we merge our government with that of the West Coast Tribal Alliance, we will control the entire Western region of this continent. However, unlike the Alliance, we are not a loosely-connected group of tribes under a treaty. We are a true vampire nation, centralized under a single leader. Therefore, my rapidly growing empire, Miss Balmont--though not yet complete--is considered by many to be the greatest structural achievement in the history of the vampire species."

My jaw practically drops straight to the crust of the Earth.

Why wasn't Angela clear about this? I just

insulted one of the most powerful leaders in our community.

I muster up the confidence to recover. "Oh, yeah, I've heard of your work-- I mean, I've heard rumors about your United Tribes even back in the city. To be honest, it's not easy getting up-to-date information about our own species where I grew up. It's the center of the human media but it's pretty much a wild jungle for vampires out there, so--"

Angela nudges me, hard.

I quickly add, "Oh, and I sincerely apologize for my ignorance, Sir Ruthven."

"I accept," he replies. "In fact, I thank you for opening my eyes to another reason for my ambitions. Your lack of awareness of our government is only one of many indications that our species remains in a dark age of our own, despite our natural strength and biological superiority. The humans, however, have thrived in establishing great mutual understandings between their nations. So long as their largest and most powerful nations mutually understand each other's ability to destroy one another, they will remain allied. We must establish a mutual understanding among our kind."

I just stare at him.

The man continues, "My goal then, I believe, should be to recover our species from the depths of disorganization and secrecy and cowardly hunting practices. If we are to become the dominant species, we must operate as the humans operate. And soon, we will--under my leadership." He pauses. "Am I boring you, Miss Balmont?"

I grab at the first smart-sounding answer. "Oh, I...

I think that's a great plan, Sir Ruthven. Actually, I'm all for the dominance of our species. It may even be the natural progression of things."

He reclines a bit on his chair with a grin. "Yes, the natural progression. I wholeheartedly agree...that we should allow our future to unfold in the natural manner, much like the humans and their hunting of other, weaker, species on this planet and their consumption of resources. That natural progression of theirs will serve as the model for us to follow. And so we shall."

I reply, "But what about the sun?"

"Do you know what the blanket in the sky is?" He speaks from the corner of his mouth while he blows a ring of smoke.

"The what?"

Angela whispers to me, "The smog."

I slap my forehead. "Oh! I've never heard it called a blanket before. But no, I don't really know exactly. I just know it's a pollutant. No one really knows what it really is, right?"

"That is where you are incorrect, Miss Balmont. It is growing to become a strong filter of ultraviolet light. And it will protect us from the sun's harmful rays for generations to come. It is the key to our advancement, to become the dominant species on Earth... We will be able to provide a workforce at all hours of the day, in every time zone." He stands up and inhales from his cigar. "I believe it was sent to protect us."

"But I thought there was no scientific data on it?"

"Scientific? No. But there is truth. You see, three of the ten tribes under my control have origins that date back long before the eldest of our surviving elders...and one of these three oldest tribes teach that The First will rise and bring our species new hope, and shield us with a blanket in the sky, and lead us to greatness. It is our destiny."

I stare at him for a moment. "Are you telling me that the smog was created by...The First?"

"I am simply informing you of my beliefs, and the beliefs of an ancient civilization. Would you not consider it a possibility that they are correct?" He blows another smoke ring with a proud posture.

I look at Angela again.

She nods with pride. "It's true, Iryna. The time is coming... It's our time to rule the world. Isn't it exciting?"

I turn back to Ruthven and ask, "So why are you telling me all this?"

His smile widens. "I have something of an offer for you, Miss Balmont. You are a very reputable young woman for your age. We all know that you are a great and powerful hunter."

"You do?"

"Do not be modest, Miss Balmont. However, despite your many achievements in this world, I see potential in you far beyond all that you have already accomplished in your short lifetime."

"I don't really know why you--"

The familiar swish of the door interrupts me.

A man enters. His large, shiny cranium distracts me almost as much as his unusually small mouth. Silently, he walks straight up to Sir Ruthven and hands him a sheet of paper.

"Thank you very much, Ivan," Ruthven mutters.

The man awkwardly exits at an unnaturally fast pace without any audible response.

"I apologize. That was my brother," Niklaus Ruthven explains with sigh. "Please excuse his lack of social prowess. He is a wonderful enforcer but sorely lacks in interpersonal skills."

I nod and hide the fact that I was more distracted by his unusual appearance. "So what exactly is this offer you've got for me?"

"We are assembling a team of covert agents to serve under my government as we expand our reach into new territories. It will be something of a secret service agency. I need attractive female agents of your unimposing size and body type for strategic purposes. Of course, your natural hunting abilities and vast experience are assets for this position. You will, however, be provided with additional training."

"Why do you think I'd be good for this though?"

"If everything they say about you is true, then you have the potential to become a major player in the future of our organization. Angela here has already signed on so you will have the opportunity to work together."

I turn to Angela. "So you wanted to get me a job in your secret service agency?"

"It's the government of the future, girl," she replies with her shoulders pulled back. "We're getting into this game at the ground level."

My gut tells me that Niklaus Ruthven is more of a salesman and politician than he is a true believer in the future of our species--let alone all that blanket stuff.

Maybe he's right. Maybe it really is time for us to take control of this planet instead of playing Trojan horse with the food's society all the time. Maybe he's even right about the whole blanket in the sky concept. But after everything I've read and heard, I don't think I can really take anyone's word for it at face value.

There's always something more--some ulterior motive--behind it all when people are trying to justify expanding their power across the world. I've read enough human history books to know that a powerful species, following an ancient belief system to justify the use of violence, has never led to anything pretty.

By the same logic of human and vampire nature, I also have a feeling I don't have much of a choice here. When a man like Ruthven makes an offer, and discloses this much information about his plans in the process, it's usually a choice between yes and death.

Angela may be naive enough to believe it all at face value, but I'm not. I know this game and I've read about it for years. It's been played for centuries.

Angela seems to be signaling something to her boss.

He nods and adds, "And, if you so choose to accept my offer... you will be assigned an apartment on the basement floor of this complex. However, since we have no available units until six months from today, you may stay with Angela in her unit for the time being."

Angela smiles like an enthusiastic, innocent little cartoon bunny.

I think back to the mold and horse radish. "Okay, I'm in."

CHAPTER 10

We shove open a large corrugated metal door into an underground warehouse-looking facility that's like nothing I've ever seen before. It's hollow with sturdy metal walls and ceilings supported by thick, shiny, columns. Angela shuts the door with a loud clank that echoes through the entire place.

Inside, a row of vampires stand side by side with a stiff, upright posture. Most of them are dressed in military fatigues. They all look to be around my age--give or take a century or two.

"Angela!" A short, little curly-haired brunette calls out. "Get your ass in here! You're late!"

Angela whispers something, to which the girl nods. Angela then announces to the entire group, "Just carry on, everyone. I'm just taking the new girl for a tour."

The loud, curly one seems to be running things around here judging by all the yelling she's doing.

It's quite the sight. If I didn't know better, I'd swear the girls were in some kind of supermodel competition with a military theme. I recognize two

ARIES BRAEBURN

of them: Bleach and Bubble. I don't see Orange anywhere in sight though.

"So this is what I'm joining?" I whisper to Angela.

"No, most of them were drafted for Ruthven's other operations. Only a few of these girls were chosen for one of our units. We get the cool black covert ops outfits after finishing basic training here. They'll give you one too, no worries."

"Who's that short, loud one?" I ask, gesturing toward the curly-haired girl who yelled at her.

"That's Agent Leigh. She does all the training stuff but she mostly works with us. Think of her as our manager. She's been in this thing since the very beginning of the recruitment process. Doesn't she just remind you of this cute little bunny that can rip your head off? She's like my idol."

The girls split into groups--their movements look so choreographed that they almost look mechanical. As soon as they start a series of drills, I recognize some basic city hunting skills on display. Compared to me, though, they're like the world-class athletes of our species. The accuracy and timing of every claw and every lunge and every step of their dash is like a dance, a very lethal dance. I'm stunned by it.

"I'm not sure I can do this," I whisper to Angela.

Agent Leigh turns around like a spinning top and screams at me, "You can do anything you put your mind to, new girl!"

Wow...I don't know about idolizing but that little girl creeps me out. Somehow, I doubt cute is the right word for her. I'd swear she's got a megaphone built into her vocal cords. I wouldn't want to be on the wrong side of her fangs.

Four feet away from us, a brunette soars through the air in attack position, heading toward Bubble. Bubble swiftly dodges and uses the attacker's own momentum to throw the brunette crashing onto a blue mat. She then launches herself into the air and pins the brunette to the ground, knee on collarbone.

Afterwards, I notice the brunette's chest area. It looks like she's got a nasty little bruise on her collarbone. That's not an easy thing to do to a vampire. I can't deny I'm just a little bit more intimidated by that scrawny little red-headed Bubble now.

Angela notices me staring at the brunette's chest area. "So, do you like what you see?"

"Umm-- what?"

"This job...you think it's worth it for moving out of that dump of yours?"

I shrug. "I guess. It's not even really a choice anymore, right? I already said I'd do it."

She winks and slaps my upper arm. "You'll get the hang of it. We need more girls like you around here."

On our way back to Angela's apartment, I suddenly feel a rush of adrenaline for no apparent reason. My head feels light and...

Thud!

I drop to the floor in the hallway, only a few feet from her apartment's door.

My head feels empty with a buzzing that won't go away. I could barely see and hear my surroundings.

She offers me her wrist with a gentle smile. "Go ahead," she whispers.

Carefully, I bite down onto the smooth skin of her

arm. Her skin sinks into her flesh against the pressure of my long, sharp fangs. Gently, I bite down a little harder and...

Pop!

The tiny little jab makes an amplified noise in my ringing head.

Her fresh, pristine blood drips slowly into my mouth. I can feel it rejuvenating me. I can feel her-- a part of me now.

I look up at her eyes...or so I try. Her head tilts back with her eyes barely open and her eyeballs rolled upward a little. Her mouth hangs open with fangs completely exposed.

She's enjoying the moment as much as I am. Somehow, I don't mind.

She helps me back into her apartment with my arm over her shoulder.

Once inside, she turns around and transforms the position into a tight, warm hug like I've never experienced before.

"Are you feeling better with a part of me inside of you now?" she asks with a little wink.

I shoot her a playful smile and stand up to my feet on my own restored strength. "Yeah. But you gotta tell me before you introduce me to some big regional leader next time, okay? I made such an ass of myself there."

"I know. Sorry, that was totally my fault." She wraps me in her arms, in another hug burrito.

"It's okay. You more than made up for it already. I can't even thank you enough for everything. Really."

She runs her hand up and down my back. She seems to slow down over the peaks and valleys of my back ribs for some reason. At first, I couldn't understand why.

"You purge, don't you?" She asks bluntly and then adds insult to injury, "You know...people around here care more about fangs than weight."

I glare at her like she had just told me the tooth fairy created the world. "Angela, just stop. I know where this is going already and I've heard it all before so--"

"No," she interrupts. "I mean it, seriously. It's really not that big of a deal to people here."

Is she seriously trying to tell me that everyone around here is more attracted to hunting ability than looks? I don't believe that for one second. Beyond that, it doesn't actually make me feel better if she lies about it like this. It's just like everyone in the city trying to sell products that tell you to believe in yourself, to stop worrying about how you look, because you'll magically be an equal to everyone else just by being delusional. It's the kind of lie that's got great intentions but works as well as a tire for a corkscrew. In the real world, we look for ways to compensate, not cover our eyes to reality. And I'm pretty sure I settled on my way of compensating even if everyone would rather hate me now.

I shove her away from me. "It's not really about that anymore. It's just me. And to answer your question...No, I don't purge."

"Don't be lying to me, girl. I thought we were getting so much closer and--"

"No, honestly, I really don't. I mean-- that's not how I do it."

"Now you totally lost me."

I let out a primal growl. "I don't feed at all. Okay,

Angela? I haven't fed for more than a year and a half. What do you think just happened in the hallway there?"

Admitting it in so many words, out loud, still feels like I'd just stripped naked in front of a crowd of strangers even though I consider her my best friend. It's just not something I ever planned to talk about--with anyone at all--so bluntly.

Even I know it's not really a secret anymore. Lots of people have known, or at least guessed it, even if I still don't really see what they're seeing when I look in the mirror. The professor sure had her suspicions, or more like assumptions, about it since the moment we met...but I never actually admitted to her in so many words. I never said it directly to anyone at all. I never had to. I guess there's a first time for everything.

Angela strokes the side of my face. "I admire that, actually. All that will power."

"Well don't. There's nothing to admire about me."

"Why? It takes a lot to do what you do, girl. I mean, damn, a whole year and a half? I could never do it. You're lucky you have that kind of will power, seriously...I mean, purging is one thing, but--"

"Lucky would be a vampire with better genes. I see them all the time, feeding on every tourist that comes into the city, and they never gain a pound of fat. The guys get muscular and the girls store it all in the right places. Me? I overfeed for one month and my upper arms get bigger than your entire butt."

"Umm, my butt isn't that--"

"I'm exaggerating, Angela. I mean, I'm not, but I-- Never mind. The point is...there's nothing to admire about me. I'm just genetically cursed."

"Sorry I'm just saying all the wrong things." She tries to pull me in for another hug, but I don't let her this time.

"No, it's not you. It's just frustrating sometimes. I'm only nineteen. Could you imagine what it'll be like when I'm like four hundred and eighty two if I start feeding again? I can run miles around the block, chasing the fittest and highest quality prey in the city. I can do it every night. My body should look perfect from doing it but, no, even then I'd look 'average'. I'd still look lazier than the vampires who spent all day leeching off the low-quality couch potato types of prey--the kind that takes about two seconds to hunt. So, I said screw it. I'll do it the only way I can...There's nothing to admire about it."

Angela's eyes are just fixated on me. I'm not quite sure if it's understanding or even pity. I think it's a little more like she's scrambling to help me but doesn't know how.

I pull her in for a hug with such a ferocious grasp that a bear would envy. Mostly, I'm just feeling a little guilty for pushing her away after seeing her face.

I try to lighten the mood, clumsily. "There wasn't much of a selection of good, healthy prey in the city anymore anyway. So I'm just being charitable now, right?"

"What do you mean?" She seems to take it seriously.

"Well things got so bad, rumor has it some of the tribes up state started building farms to grow their own healthy livestock. So, if you think about it, I was just being charitable to the other vampires in the city by not competing with them."

"Well, this ain't the city. And if I'm gonna be a good host to you around these parts, I ain't letting you miss out on the local West Coast flavors."

"Angela. Did you hear a single word I--"

"I get it," she interrupts. "But I'm gonna show you a better way to do it. You can get the best of both worlds, girl."

I'm not sure what she's getting at but I don't feel too comfortable about anything she seems to be implying.

She kneels in front of me and analyzes the wound on my ribs.

"Okay, what are you doing this time?" I ask, slightly worried.

She grabs my midsection.

Her hands nearly wrap around my entire waist like a belt. I think to myself, my waist can't be that tiny, can it? It must be her hands. I mean, I know I still need to lose more weight--I just know it.

"Here, let me teach you a little trick of mine," she begins. "I used to do it myself all the time back when I was like you."

"Umm, wait. What's this trick for?"

"Just watch." She pats the side of my waist and gently places her fingernail over my open wound. "Okay, when you're alone, just squeeze...and squeeze out as much as you can, as fast as you can. You gotta do it fast though, so your eyes jump into focus and you'd know to stop right then. If you just go and let it bleed like normal, you'll just kill yourself eventually 'cause your eyes will never trigger like that."

"I don't get what you mean though. The eyes

jumping into focus thing--how do I know when to stop?"

"You gotta stop the moment you feel that sudden jerk, that natural high in your head. You know, like when you're hunting some really fit prey."

"Oh, you mean the adrenaline rush spike when there's a sudden loss of blood?"

"Yeah, whatever you call it. But you gotta stop like that very moment though, or you'll just drop dead if you go too far."

"Okay, I think I get it. I don't know if I'll really--"

"It's an art, girl. Get it down and it'll be as easy as hunting a bike-riding prey."

I shake my head and look down. "I'm just a product of everything that's wrong with life. I'm disgusting in so many ways."

Quietly, she responds, "No. You really aren't and I'm gonna prove it."

Angela takes me down the hallway from her apartment. Holding onto my hand tightly, she leads me around a corner I'd never turned before and into a stairwell that goes even deeper into the ground.

"I thought you lived on the bottom floor," I remark.

"I do." She winks with her adorable smile. "But no one lives down here."

We duck under thick, rusted pipes that weave around each other like a three dimensional maze. Flickering lighting illuminates only about a quarter of this vast boiler room level.

After a few maneuvers under the larger and smaller pipes, we reach a dark corner where the main lights seem to have burnt out already. All that's left are two spotlights with black covers, an arrangement of candles on the floor, and a couple of wooden boxes.

"What are you gonna do, sacrifice me?" I nudge her with a half grin.

"We're going to do something special," she whispers as she gently pushes me toward the middle of the candle arrangement. "Relax, girl. You know I won't ever hurt you. Tilt your head a little."

"Umm, okay." I carefully tilt my head in the opposite direction that I did for the vendor girl. The bite marks are probably healed by now if my immune system still functions like a healthy vampire, but I rather not take the risk and provoke more questions.

She rubs the skin on my neck with her finger tip and places her wrist less than an inch from my mouth. "Have you done this before?"

"Done what?" I sound a little shaky.

"Relax. You trust me, right?"

"Yeah, Angela. Of course I trust you."

"Okay, bite into my wrist at the same time I bite into your neck. It's just like feeding on the prey but we're doing it to each other at the same time so blood's gonna cycle through us, back and forth, like we're one person. It's a trust thing around here...they call it a love loop."

"But it takes half an hour to digest through the liver and then it--"

She shoves her wrist into my mouth with a smile. "Don't ruin it, smart girl. Just try it. I promise you won't gain an ounce from it."

Silently, I close my eyes and carefully bite down onto her wrist. At the same time, I feel her fangs land onto my neck. They sink through my skin, smoothly. It feels like nothing I've ever felt before--I get it. We feel so connected, at a level I never dreamed of. Our lives are in each other's hands. We trust each other in a moment of--

"Ow!" She shrieks.

I pull away and wipe the blood dripping from my lips. "What? What happened? Did I do it wrong?"

"Damn, girl. I'm not food. You gotta do it gently!"

"I'm so sorry. Honestly, I've never done this before so I just--"

She smiles and runs her finger over my lips. "It's okay, don't worry about it. I know it's your first time."

Disappointed but unscathed, she guides my body carefully into a dramatic gesture pose.

Methodically going through the rest of her motions, she retrieves a lighter from one of the two wooden boxes and lights up each of the candles on the floor. She then switches on one of the spotlights.

"What's all this for?" I ask her, finally.

"I told you I was gonna prove you're not disgusting, right? Well I'm gonna draw you and show you in black and white, so you can't argue."

And so I hold the pose--for the next twenty minutes...and another after that. I've never seen anyone look as happy as she does now so I figure it's a good thing.

I've never felt so close to anyone before and I never expected to in all of eternity. I don't regret one second of coming here. It was all worth it.

CHAPTER 11

Courtney shoves me away after our nightly ritual, like yesterday's garbage. She lets out a bored sigh.

"Just come with us, will you?" I ask with a shred of hope. "You know what it took to convince the doctor to go through with this, don't you?"

"Ugh. I don't care if you were one of them, boy. You don't have to, like, waste time making deals with the food. Besides, it's gonna be...boring."

If there's one thing I've learned from Courtney, it's that she's not faking when she blends in with the younger generations. I don't think that brain of hers has aged a second in the last century. I guess a few hundred years from now, if and when she finally mingles with elders, she might finally grow up on the inside.

"It won't be boring," I argue.

The elevator slowly begins to move upward like molasses on a humid summer night.

The doctor and I check our reflections in the mirrors to either side. We're surrounded by humans, dressed in suits. One of them is a female too. How the world changed between two major stock market crashes.

The stench of over-priced coffee is drowning out their appetizing scent. I know where the doctor's instincts are leading him, but I'm not sure what I crave more: the sugar in their coffee or the blood in their veins.

A human woman with a puffy mop of hair glances at me. I nod politely.

An automated female voice calls out, "Fifty seventh floor."

"Are we almost there yet?" the doctor whispers with a smirk. His sense of humor takes time to adjust to but we've got more than enough.

"You know, when we're around--" I cough twice. "Let's be more normal, okay?"

The woman glares at me like flames are ready to burst out of her eyes. It takes me a minute to realize that she probably thought I was referring to her gender. Given the circumstances, I'm not about to explain that I was talking about her entire species.

"How is Courtney?" the doctor asks.

"She's...the same as always. There's this new girl in class though. She's a hard one to talk to but I haven't felt this way since--"

"Is she...one of us?"

"Umm--" I hesitate and glance at the human woman out of fear. "She's a, umm...pure."

The doctor sighs. "You know, you cannot have children with a pure blood, son. You must find one like yourself if you are to continue your blood line."

The big-haired woman drops her jaw in shock and

disapproval.

"Seventy-fourth floor," the sexy elevator voice announces to us.

The doctor and I exit the elevator--quickly, in my case.

Recounting our conversation from the human woman's point of view, she probably thinks I'm a sexist human with a strangely reversed-racist father. She doesn't know he meant it literally-- turned vampires, born human, can't reproduce with pure blood vampires and that's what he meant to say. Maybe I should be glad he didn't go ahead and say it in so many words.

We walk through a maze of marble hallways until a young female human opens a set of double-doors for us. She nods nervously. She probably knows what we are. I try to give her a reassuring smile, but I can't be sure if she'll take it as a seductive hunting glare.

Inside, Mr. Wolfe closes the blinds of his large plate glass window. His stubby gray beard adds a touch of wisdom to those gray eyes of his. He would make an intimidating-looking vampire. That is, if he weren't wearing a thick makeshift metal collar like he is now.

"Welcome, Doctor Thornton," Wolfe greets. He turns to me and asks, "And you are...?"

"Adrian. Adrian Thornton is the name I go by in your world now," I answer.

He nods. "Make yourselves at home." He strokes the collar. "I hope you are not offended by my...precautions."

"Not at all," the doctor responds with a fang-baring

smile.

"Now...I understand that you are proposing an agreement on behalf of your...vampire species. Is that an offensive term?"

"No, that is a correct term." The doctor nods. "However, we can no more represent our entire species than you can represent yours. We are simply proposing an agreement between your multi-national human corporation and my Tribal Alliance, which consists of eleven of the Western region's vampire communities."

Wolfe strolls around the room with his hands behind his back. "What is the percentage of your Alliance's over those of your kind in this country?"

"We do not formally recognize your national borders, Mister Wolfe. Within this region, the Tribal Alliance was formed under a treaty between more than fifty percent of the tribes in the entire region."

"And your...opposition? I believe you mentioned an opposition government of some sort within your region."

I speak up. "Don't worry about our opposition. He's reckless and ambitious but he doesn't know what he's doing."

Wolfe stops in his tracks. "Am I to believe that this opposition of yours will not attack my corporation's properties if I am to sign your agreement?"

I shrug casually. "He might try...but we believe our Alliance's member tribes will show more loyalty to us than the United Tribes will show to their leader."

The doctor clears his throat. "With the help of your corporation and its worldwide reach, we will be better equipped as a government to enforce our policies over those of our opposition. That, Mister

Wolfe, will be the key to our shared prosperity in an uncertain future."

Wolfe nods and promptly signs our agreement in a major step for our civilization and a daunting step toward conflict with the United Tribes.

Back in the elevator, the female voice counts down as we descend. We're alone this time, thankfully.

"How'd you do that?" I ask curiously.

"The key to human business is to transform your own goal into something that the human desires. To sell a product, convince the human that your product will cause it to find beautiful women and care-free celebration. They have used it on their own kind for generations and are quite stupid and easily manipulated by the technique even today."

"Hey, I used to be one of--"

"No offense intended, son."

"Well, you think we can really pull it off though? You think we can really over-power Ruthven's people with Wolfe's company?"

"The agreement was your suggestion, Adrian. My words were only the means of persuasion. I will capitalize on opportunities as they present themselves and the illnesses seem to be spreading beyond borders. For now, we wait."

Adrian Thornton

CHAPTER 12

lass begins like any other lecture--on any other night. After a crash course in Ruthven's covert ops program, it seems like routine is beginning to kick in for me.

"Hey, Irene." A plaid-wearing girl smiles at me.

Sadly enough, I don't even know her name yet...I'd feel like an idiot if I correct her now.

I haven't improved much on the socializing front, but I feel like a little bit less of an outsider now. Maybe it's just from knowing I'm part of something so supposedly significant. I feel good today.

In fact, I'd even say I feel confident and adventurous today...enough so to strategically take a seat right next to the boy I was drawn to since my first day in the professor's class. I still doubt he likes me but I've learned how to secure government information. So I think it's about time I find out his name--or at least dare to try.

He doesn't seem to notice me at all this time.

He just turns away from me and whispers something to Orange. I don't see Bleach and Bubble anywhere in the circle. I wonder why Orange bothered to come to class at all if her friends are skipping.

It never ceases to amaze me, no matter how much I absorb about the history and psychology, of both humans and our kind, I'm still a bumbling idiot when it comes to dealing with real life.

In the world according to Iryna, learning to spy on political opponents is easier than talking to someone you find attractive. How pathetic am I?

Professor Marsden enters the circle and the entire class quiets down.

I notice she looks even more serious than usual. Did someone get caught cheating? Did someone copy off my test? Did I accidentally hand in the wrong paper?

"Students," she begins, "normally, I would begin today with the fun facts of fundamental attribution error, and all its wonderful effects on our behavior patterns... However--"

I notice a few students in the class shuffling and shifting in their places. Judging by the way the professor kicked things off today, they're probably ready to go home for the day.

The boy is starting to pack up too. Crap, I think to myself. Just when I got the best seat in the circle, I only get to keep it for about two minutes...and I didn't even get to ask his name.

"You may want to hear this announcement, Adrian," the professor informs him with a somber expression.

I stop in my tracks like a giant, flashing, neon sign had just been slammed into my face. I ask myself, *Wait, did I hear that right? Could it really be?*

Quickly, I muster up a chunk of bravery and whisper to him, "Your name is...Adrian?"

He nonchalantly nods to me and turns his full attention back to the professor.

Still, I rejoice in my head.

And then it hits me. I've got an awkward smile pasted across my face while a storm of epiphany ripples through my mind. Worst of all, I'm still staring at him.

Adrian turns to me again. I quickly pull back into an awkward frown as if I'm imitating some old toothless human with an under-bite.

He turns to Orange again and whispers to her. Why does he keep leaning in toward her like that? What can he possibly see in her?

She cracks a wide, open, confident smile with her canines exposed. Her fangs are short, subtle and slightly rounded. They barely look sharp enough to bite into a vegetable, let alone the skin and flesh of living prey.

And then it finally dawns on me.

Angela wasn't being creative with her wording when she told me that people around here care more about fangs than body shape. Apparently, she meant it, literally: fangs are an important trait of attractiveness in this community.

It all makes sense now. This Orange girl seems to be about as stupid as my big toe yet she's got some big regional leader's son acting all close with her? It's got to be the fangs.

Right away, I feel hopelessly compelled to hide my long, sharp primal fangs with my lips pulled in like a human with missing teeth. It almost lacerates the inside of my lips but I don't care. I just managed to discover a whole new insecurity about my anatomy...and all it took was one person to hammer it in.

And then the professor announces a piece of news that makes me feel petty and utterly stupid for every thought that had just crossed my mind...

She announces to the class, "Sir Niklaus Ruthven's United Tribes have taken control of three of the largest human metropolitan centers on the West Coast. According to my sources, his plan is to invade additional human cities as the opportunity presents itself. His forces are systematically attacking the communications networks and local leaderships before hunting down the common prey. The human national leaders have been completely disconnected from the occupied cities."

What the hell?

Apparently, my boss went ahead and did something of this scale without even notifying his supposedly-elite-forces about it? Agent Leigh and Angela never mentioned a word about this and neither did our Commander in Chief himself. Why were we kept in the dark? Worse, what does he have in store for us?

Adrian whispers to Orange, "Ruthven's just gonna get us all killed, that reckless idiot. My father just made a deal with the--"

Orange replies, "But doesn't your dad still, like, own most of the tribes?"

"Well he runs more than half of the West Coast, yeah. But he united his tribes under peaceful agreements...he didn't shove them all under his command the way Ruthven did. That's exactly why my father would never agree to sign a treaty with him. That jackass is gonna start World War Three and he doesn't even know it yet."

I nervously tap Adrian on his shoulder. "So, who's your father again?"

"Doctor Thornton," he answers impatiently. He barely even looks at me before he turns back to the fruit-colored creature.

"So there's, like, seven tribes, right?" Orange asks him.

"There's *eleven* in my dad's Tribal Alliance," Adrian patiently answers as he leans in even closer to her. "There's gonna be twenty-one after he reasons with the sub-leaders of Ruthven's tribes."

The professor glances at her notes. "There are unconfirmed reports from the Mid-Western tribes that the humans have begun to launch their own attacks overseas...and they appear to be targeting their own brothers and sisters--the ones in other major human nations."

Adrian asks, "So the humans think it's their own species that's attacking their cities? I knew it. I saw it coming."

"It is not confirmed but it appears to be so, Adrian. It seems that their national leaders believe they are defending their own soil from overseas threats...when they are in fact aggressively launching an international war."

"Why can't they, like, even get along with their own kind?" Orange remarks with her nose flared out.

"Like we're any different," Adrian mutters under his breath.

The professor replies to Orange, "Yes, it is unfortunate, but there are more alarming dangers at the forefront now than their social development. Once the human national leaders learn that the city invaders are not human, they will naturally retaliate on Ruthven's occupying forces without mercy. As a result, if they discover the nature of their attackers, they will most likely target all members of our species--even those who are not affiliated with Niklaus Ruthven and his United Tribes."

I join the discussion. "You think they'll attack their own cities?"

"There is no telling how they will respond if entire cities are overrun by our fang-baring peers. Nothing is set in stone. The East Coast tribes have not yet communicated with our United Tribes in any way." She turns and announces to the entire class, "However, to be safe, those of you who have family members hunting or vacationing in the cities may be excused from class. We will review last week's material for the remainder of the class and attendance will be optional until further notice."

"Wait... Why did Ruthven do it *now*, of all times?" An older, scruffy-looking student asks. "Why did he choose tonight to launch the attack?"

"To*day*," Marsden corrects him, "the attacks occurred during the day."

"How is that possible?"

The professor flips through her notes. "Sir Ruthven ordered the attacks as soon as his research department confirmed that the...so-called blanket in the sky...the pollutant, was deemed ready to be used to his advantage in more than eighty five percent of the West Coast."

"To be used?" Orange asks with a blank-looking

curiosity on her face. "Used for what?"

"...To be used for protection from the sun, dear."

Suddenly, it feels like there's no time to be nineteen anymore. My petty personal problems and minor victories are overshadowed by the reality that's around all of us.

Today, it's officially safe for us to walk the Earth, day and night, without fear of severe burns from the sun's ultraviolet light rays. It turns out Sir Niklaus Ruthven was right after all--at least about what the smog does for us--even if the how and why may still be up for debate.

If the humans were, in fact, responsible for the smog in the sky then their own industrial progress has ironically caused their own downfall after thousands of years as the dominant species on this planet.

Historians of the future will say that the events that took place today were a pivotal turning point in the progress of our species.

I can picture it already: Vampires around the world will celebrate today's date as an inter-regional holiday, the day on which we effectively claimed our place at the top of the social food chain. They'll write about it as a day of triumph and victory over our evolutionary predecessors. They'll write stories and gloat over their victory at the expense of the species whose culture, language, and biology shaped what we are today.

Personally, I have no illusions about what really happened today.

Back when I read the human history soap operas for fun, I felt somehow disconnected from it all.

Subconsciously, I almost thought of the historical leaders and countries as distant, fictitious characters. At the time, no one in our species had ever carried the burden of running an entire nation, or making decisions that would affect an entire company's workforce. Even the regional tribe populations are dwarfed by the sheer number of living beings that were under the control of the human leaders.

I don't know if Ruthven's going to stay in power, or if Thornton would even be a better leader. All I know is that most of us are just trying to get by in this community and in this world in general. We're not giving the orders but we'll come to feel, and be held, just as responsible for the destruction today as Niklaus Ruthven himself.

The way I see it, today won't go down in our true history as a victory for us. It's the day we begin to feel what it's like to carry the responsibility of being the dominant species in this world.

Humanity had its chance. Now, it's our turn...and we're probably not ready for it.

CHAPTER 13

Over the next two weeks, Angela and I are two of the five to ten students who still show up for every single class. Adrian shows up about once or twice a week but that's pretty much it. Most of the others must have either gone to be with their families--or are using that as their universal excuse to skip classes.

I know we don't have to show up. After all, the Ruthven attacks--and the human leaders' reactions to them and to each other--have given us more excuses to skip class than a million clear, sunny days. But a part of me wants to pick the professor's brain for knowledge and wisdom especially now that we're at the edge of anarchy.

Anyone who grew up in the human-influenced culture of the city would call me a nerd for thinking this way. They'd say only a geek would still come to class every day if there wasn't any reason to. They might be right--but most of them have been wiped clean off the face of this planet now, by their own kind no less, so I'll look for a second opinion.

The professor is one of the only people who can still keep my mind sharp, whether it's in class or in some random debate outside. We get into discussions that make me think critically and push me to find new directions. My mind gets to evolve and I might need that in the new world to come.

As for why Angela continues to come to class, that's a whole other question. I have no idea, really.

She seems to be absorbing most of the class material but I don't think she has any idea what we're talking about when get into our philosophical debates. I can just imagine the gears in her head clanking and overheating when the professor and I start debating.

Worse, every single time Adrian is in class with us, I find myself talking a lot less and looking a lot more like a toothless elder with my lips wrapped over my over-sized fangs.

After class on a relatively typical Friday night under the world circumstances, the professor pulls me aside for a talk.

She begins, "I have noticed your pattern of behavior of late, Iryna. Would you like to discuss it?"

The truth is: no, not really. If she's talking about what I think she's talking about, I really don't want to discuss it with her at all. I'd rather talk about something, anything, but that.

I reply, "Aren't there bigger problems in the world right now?"

"Yes...but you must address your problems at home before you can begin to solve the many problems abroad. I have always seen great potential in you, dear."

"Fine, what is it?" I shrug with a sigh.

"You remind me very much of myself, my younger self from centuries ago. In almost every society to which I have had to adjust, especially in my first four centuries, I had developed new reasons to despise my own biological makeup. At times, I was too pale, too tall--even too thin. Often times, the measures we have to take to meet the dominant standards are far more tolling on our psychic makeup than one would expect at first."

"But it's not really about that for me, not even when I lived in the city. I mean, at first, it sort of was, but--"

"At first--continue on that line of thought. What were you thinking in the beginning?"

"Well, I knew I wanted a mate because a part of me craved that closeness, that bond. And I guess I still do. I never had it until I was fifteen."

"So you believed that your appearance was the reason you could not attain this goal?"

"Well, no...Not really. I mean not rationally, at least. He probably had a million other reasons to leave me by then anyway, even if they were all coming from his own delusions. But I guess, from the start, I felt like it always made it that much harder to get what I needed as much as everyone else. I mean, look at that orange-tanned girl. What the hell can anyone see in an idiot like her?"

"Do not be so quick to judge, dear. Remember, the confirmation bias topic we had discussed in class. Not everything in life can be accurately observed in third-person view without knowing the other person's points of view. The recent generations prefer to simplify in order to understand a situation or a concept but that is not always a path to the truth. Sometimes, there are many layers to the whole truth...and to oversimplify it would be to misunderstand it."

"Is that a fancy way of saying she's probably great in bed?"

"I am speaking in general, Iryna. Even if Adrian truly had been as shallow as you assume, the real problem is that you are already acting under the assumption that he is. You do not know for certain yet you are dooming yourself to a fate created by your own beliefs. You will create a self-fulfilling prophecy if you continue down this road."

"Yeah, yeah, I get it...but it's not just that. I just think if I can look the way I do on the inside, none of this would be an issue. Maybe I'll shave my fangs down. Or maybe if I was dumber and just painted myself orange--"

"Have you given any thought to why our society is the way it is? By that, I mean the standards of attractiveness."

I tilt my head and shrug. "I don't really care. It is what it is so why's it even matter why? All I know is I wasn't naturally built to fit into the ideals, so maybe I just wasn't meant to survive in it. Back in the city, I struggled to keep my weight down. Here, I've got long, sharp fangs. Let's face it: Maybe I'm like one of the mistakes in nature's production line. I'm a defective unit and I got rejected by all the consumers in every market. Maybe it's nature's way of telling me that I'm the end of the road for my family's stock of crap genes. So there, you'da been right all along: maybe I really am supposed to die before three hundred."

She takes a deep breath, pulling air down to the bottom of her lungs. "I am sure you find comfort in believing that everything is either meant to be or not meant to be. The truth is: we create our own paths, dear. It is a matter of taking responsibility."

I smirk and roll my eyes. "Yeah, okay. I must have chosen to have giant fangs and a huge appetite. Excuse me if I forgot the day I got that menu."

"No, but you may have other attributes that may already be attractive to your potential mate. Each and every one of us has shortcomings to overcome as well as advantages at our disposal--some are more obvious to the naked eye than others. You are only looking to appeal to one mate, not an entire civilization. It may be that you already possess the qualities that your potential mate desires."

"Do you believe in fate?" I ask. She doesn't quite answer but the look in her eyes tells me it's not a concept that fits well into her objective and analytical view of the world. Or maybe it just bothers her that it's something she has yet to explain to herself after so many years in this world, and she would rather not talk about it. Either way, she trails off with a non-answer while I consider the possibility of fate for the first time in years.

Long after the professor leaves, I lean against the willow tree by myself. I need a break from the chaos and a nice quiet moment alone is all I need.

My eye lids begin to fall as I imagine a peaceful emptiness with water flowing toward smog-free mountains.

"Iryna!" Angela yells. "Get your ass up! We gotta talk--right now!"

"Whoa... What's wrong?" I smile at the sight of her, expecting a smile in return like she usually gives me.

Instead, she grabs hold of my arm and violently pulls me up to my feet. I figure she has a good reason for being so urgent. Maybe she has family members in the occupied cities...or maybe she has issues with her boss.

Whatever it is, it must be big, judging by the look of panic in her face...

"Stay away from that Adrian boy, you got that?" She yells. "He's bad news, girl. Trust me. You don't wanna get mixed up with these political types."

"Umm...Aren't you in Ruthven's secret service thing?"

"That's different. That's..." She hesitates and shakes it off. "Nevermind. Forget it. It's too complicated. But just trust me, okay? Promise me, now. Promise me you won't talk to him ever again."

"Well, I don't think that'd be too hard. I mean, he doesn't even seem to like me. I've got giant tusks and he just wants Orange's tiny little bumps. It's my stupid hunter genes."

A look of relief comes over Angela's face.

She finally smiles back at me with the same enthusiasm that I'd gotten used to. If I didn't know better I might even think it's a smile of satisfaction, of a job well done.

I guess she's just that relieved.

Adrian must have really hit a nerve with her at some point. My guess is it's more personal than political. Maybe she knows something I don't.

CHAPTER 14

he western clearing was probably a beautiful place to just sit and stare at the natural scenery before the smog came. Sometimes, when I stand at the west end of the forest, I can almost--just almost--see the outlines of the white-tipped mountain tops far on the horizon. It doesn't happen often though, and the way things are going, we'll probably be seeing less and less of views like that.

I randomly decide to take a peaceful walk around the surrounding areas. All I've seen of the entire Western Regions so far is the forest and the route from the train station we arrived at. Just out of curiosity, I want to see what else I'd find if I wander around a little.

The smog seems especially thick today. Maybe it really is getting thicker or maybe I just picked a bad day for my futile attempt at sightseeing...but I'm a stubborn little vampire being. I'm not letting that stop me.

I find a row of three cabins by the shore. They're much smaller than the exterior of Ruthven

Apartments but maybe someone built a few underground facilities with a similar idea in mind.

I pick the first one and snoop around on the porch for a bit.

I stop and check around first. There doesn't seem to be anyone around for miles. It's quiet and secluded. Judging by the lack of light or sounds on the inside, it's probably empty inside too.

I crack a window open and...I couldn't get it open any wider than it already is. It's stuck. I figure, since I've come this far, I might as well go all the way. I slide in through the small opening. I'm surprised I fit through this way but I do.

It's dark inside. I tense up my eyes and get a little night vision going.

It's definitely not anything like Ruthven's building. There are no stone walls or stairs down to a high tech underground level, just old fashioned human furnishings with the heads of a few horned animals on the walls.

I couldn't help but think to myself, what kind of species calls us hell spawn in their fiction and then goes around hanging decapitated heads on their own walls? It's a little disturbing, really.

I reach up and stroke the end of a horn. It feels real.

I turn around...two large men are standing over me. They look to be about six feet tall, probably taller. One of them seems to be missing all his teeth and has an egg-shaped frame about him. The other one has more hair on him than any other animal I've ever seen.

I take in a whiff of their foul odor... They're my kind, I'm ashamed to say. They've vampires. Maybe

I blamed the wrong species.

"Oh! Hi," I greet them with a nervous smile. "Is this your place?"

"This whole region is ours, little lady," the toothless one replies.

"Yeah, breaking and entering ain't acceptable in this community," the hairy one adds.

I back away toward the opened window. "Hey, I work for Sir Ruthven too, so no harm done, right? I'll just head out and--"

The hairy one grabs my wrist. "Where's your I.D. then, little government lady?"

"Umm, I-- I don't have one. I'm a--" I try to explain.

"Oh, you must be part of a super-special secret service agency!" The toothless one exclaims.

I breathe out a sigh of relief. They figured it out, I can relax now.

"Yeah," the hairy one replies, "Ol' Niklaus must be hiring little runway model rejects with big sharp fangs to work as his bodyguards now! She's *just* wide enough to catch a small bullet!"

The two men break out into uncontrollable laughter.

I glance at them both in the eyes. "Seriously? You really don't get it?"

"What's there to get?" The toothless one continues to belch out laughter.

"Covert operations? Missions where people won't ever see us coming?" I shrug.

"Yeah, sure." They both continue to laugh.

I can easily pull my wrist out of the hairy man's grip but I don't bother. Not yet. I know I can take them both.

Suddenly, I hear a familiar voice. "Let her go."

It's Adrian. What's he doing here? How'd he find me?

The hairy one recognizes him. "Hey, this ain't none of your business, Junior."

"Well, see, that girl you're holding there... She's a friend of mine. So the way I see it, you made it my business now."

While Adrian is distracted by the hairy one, the toothless man sneakily walks around him and punches him in the kidneys.

Adrian folds over like an accordion.

I grab the hairy man's wrist and jab my knuckle into his neck, right below the jaw bone. He lets go of me and takes a moment to recover from choking and struggling for air.

I remember a move from Agent Leigh's training class... I slide across the floor and sweep the toothless man's ankles out from under him with a scissor motion.

Just as the toothless man lands, I see in the corner of my eye, for a split second, that the hairy one is about ready again.

So I flip around, jump off of the toothless man's face and use his nose as a springboard. With a crack, I launch myself into the air... And I jab my knee cap into the hairy man's throat.

He falls to the ground like a tree.

I smirk. "So, anyone still wanna see my I.D.?"

The two big men run out of the cabin faster than squirrels from a Siberian husky.

"Whoa...That was amazing!" Adrian exclaims as he gets up to his feet. "Where'd you learn to do all that? Were you serious about the whole..."

I dive onto him. "Don't worry about it... But

thanks for saving me... Or, I mean, trying to save me."

"You're amazing, you know that?" He pulls me in closer, and tilts his head...

Angela dives onto my hips and tears me out of the comfort of my dreams. It feels like she just cracked my back in the process.

I rub my eyes and welcome myself back into boring, old reality.

"Wake the hell up, girl!" She yells.

I roll over and muster up the breath to talk. "Ugh. Come on, Angela. It's two o'clock in the afternoon. Go back to sleep like a normal vampire being, will you?"

"No, this is important!" She yanks me by my arm and drags my body off the bed. "Come on! This is gonna be huge!"

I force myself to yawn a few times just to moisten up my eyes. I still can't quite see where I'm going.

"Change into uniform," she practically commands me at the opposite end of the apartment.

"Hey, you think Agent Leigh would teach us some kind of hyper vampire-amplified martial arts or something?" I ask, still groggy.

"Just shut up and get changed, girl. He wanted to talk to us like fifteen minutes ago!"

I change as fast as I could. It's not so much a uniform as it is just a black skin-tight bodysuit. If my fantasies come true, maybe we'll do some kind of ninja espionage in these deathly uncomfortable things.

We head out into the hallway.

"What were you dreaming about anyway?" Angela

asks.

"Umm... Just some guys trying to attack me in a cabin."

"But I heard you say something about saving you...did someone save you?"

"Well no, more like tried to save me... In my dream, Agent Leigh taught us these really cool moves, and inside, I actually knew how to do it all. It was like second nature, sort of like when you dream you can speak a language that you don't really know in real life. So I ended up kicking these two hick guys' butts all by myself."

"So someone tried to save you, right? Who was it?"

"...You." I smile innocently. "You were so sweet. You didn't want them to hurt me even though I could handle them all by myself."

She smiles back like I'd just told her she was the greatest friend in the world. To be honest, I'm only still smiling because I'm re-living what I really dreamt about.

Inside the leader's apartment, Niklaus Ruthven sits behind his desk with a glass of wine in hand, as usual. Only this time, there are two men standing right behind him.

"My beautiful agents," Sir Ruthven begins, "I trust you have already been introduced to my brothers, Ivan and Donat."

I had no idea Donat was related to them. Thinking back, he must have moved out of the community-funded place after his brother became leader. He probably lives in this complex now.

Angela nods to them both but Donat smiles directly at me, and just me.

Ivan stands motionless like a living, breathing

security camera. He observes us with those beady little eyes, without a single hint of emotion. His strangely tiny little mouth is shut. I wonder if the man even needs to feed or breathe. He sends chills down my spine.

Ruthven continues, "I have a top secret mission of utmost importance for the both of you. It will be something of a test of character, and of your will to survive--to be a part of an organization run by the strong and brave."

Immediately, my mind begins to wander into the possibilities. Maybe he really will get Agent Leigh to teach us some cool Hollywood ninja moves. I start to picture myself saving Adrian from some big, evil attacker and probably look more distracted than I should in front of the boss.

"Take a seat," Ruthven tells us.

After Angela and I take our seats across from his desk, I begin to feel a little more nervous about the whole thing. What is this test? What if it's nothing like my dreams but more like some grueling assignment where we have to hunt down hundreds and hundreds of targets? I don't think I'm ready.

Slowly, he lights a cigar. I'd swear he likes to delay just to keep the suspense up and make himself feel superior.

Involuntarily, I glance over at Ivan again. There's something about that man. It's like the feeling I get when I know there's another city female behind me, watching my every move as I walk down the street, ready to break my arms, just to compete for our next carcass. I've yet to hear Ivan speak a single word, come to think of it.

Angela nudges me and glares at me. I think she

means to tell me to stop staring at the big man's brother like a caged animal.

I gather myself and turn back to the boss.

"It has come to my attention," the leader begins, "that the South-Western tribes have demonstrated an unacceptably low percentage of believers in The First."

"The First?" I ask.

In the corner of my eye, I can see Angela is shooting me another glare.

He explains, "The First is the creator of our blanket in the sky, Agent Balmont."

"Oh... right."

He blows a giant smoke ring. "Our ancient belief system is an integral part of the progress of the Western regions as a world power. It is the key to our advancement as the new government of this area."

"So...you're sending us to preach to them?"

"No, Agent Balmont, I am sending the two of you to take control of the remainder of the region. It is our destiny to administer the government of the entire region, and if necessary, we will reach our destiny by force."

I squint. "Doesn't that kind of defeat the purpose of a--"

Angela jabs me in the side with her elbow. I get it and immediately shut up.

Niklaus Ruthven blows another ring of smoke into the air and leans in closer to us. "Your mission is to infiltrate the headquarters of Doctor Thornton, and to eliminate the opposition leader."

My heart begins to race but I try as hard as I can to hold it back and slow it down. In all the grueling training exercises I've had to do, none of them remotely compare to this moment.

"Wait," I reply with hesitation, "are you telling us to assassinate Doctor Thornton?"

"A rose by any other name, Agent Balmont. I am simply ordering the two of you to deliver our administration to our rightful destiny. That is all." He inhales from the cigar again as if he needs to refuel himself.

I pull in a deep breath of the leader's second-hand smoke. "I'm sorry but-- I mean, with all due respect, sir, aren't there a million more experienced and more trained agents to do this job? I mean, at least in my case...I'm practically new."

"I have issued you an order, not an offer. However, your reputation being what it is, I will explain my government's situation plainly."

"...My reputation?"

"I have spent large amounts of my United Tribes' resources to acquire, train, and test many of my agents. You, on the other hand, are simply a discovery--a fortunate discovery. You are naturally able yet you are a low cost asset. I feel that you have already shown that you are capable of completing this mission."

"I appreciate how highly you think of me...but you're sending the two of us to go up against the entire headquarters of Thornton's people?"

"No. My brothers, Ivan and Donat, will be in charge of clearing the way for your infiltration. Ivan will disable the core security systems and Angela will eliminate the guards. Your task, Agent Balmont, is simple and unmistakable. Eliminate Doctor Thornton and report back to Ivan and

Donat. Is that clear enough?"

"Yes, sir." My nerves start to act up.

It's all sinking in: I'm being ordered to assassinate Adrian's father, and like he said, it's an order, not an offer. He won't let me live if I say no. I get it.

The truth is the only thing I'm trying to think of is a way to tell someone on the outside about all this, and then stop it from happening. If anything, I should be the ultimate double-agent right now for Ruthven's opposition. I'm just not completely sure who the good guys are right now but I know what Ruthven is ordering me to do can't be right.

I guess if I find a way to help Thornton, he'd be the better choice simply because I don't already know for sure that he's this much of a murdering, scheming deceiver. Sadly enough, that's the best anyone could ask for in a politician--who knows what'll happen after he takes over.

"My brothers will escort you to the location in four hours," Ruthven adds. "The doctor will be sound asleep in the daylight." He stands up and blows a ring of smoke. "As you understand, this is a top secret operation of a sensitive nature. If any information should reach the wrong hands, both of you will be held accountable. Is that understood?"

"Yes, sir," Angela answers with her shoulders pulled back proudly.

I nervously answer, "Yes, Sir."

CHAPTER 15

ack at Angela's apartment, I keel over on the edge of her bed and cradle my head with my palms.

"I can't do this," I grumble under my breath.

"What's wrong this time?" Angela asks with a tone of disapproval.

"I said I can't do this, Angela. I can't go and kill a man! His son is in our class. What's wrong with you people?"

"You didn't have no problem ripping out the hearts of an entire tribe in the Central Regions, girl. What happened to you?"

"What? I never killed a whole tribe." I stand up and unzip my uniform.

"Why are you changing? We're leaving in... like less than three hours now."

"I-- I just need to get out of this thing for a bit." I shrug casually. The truth is, I need an excuse to get out of here and talk to the others about this whole mess, but I can't do it in this skin-tight covert ops uniform.

She moves in closer and runs her hand up and down my upper arm, gently. "It's okay, girl. You can tell me the truth. You trust me, right?"

"I've never even killed another vampire...well, before the one in your fridge."

She smiles. "It's okay. I understand how hard it is to admit it. I really do."

Our eyes meet for a moment.

I think she's having a close-friends moment but I'm just confused right now. Why does she insist that I killed a whole tribe in the Central Regions? I've never even been there. The closest I've been to the area is feeling the bumps of the railway tracks on my way here with Professor Marsden.

Angela rubs my back. "It's alright. I understand you in so many ways, girl."

That's good, I think to myself, *because I don't understand one bit of what she's implying or what she's thinking.*

Still, there's a childlike innocence in her face that somehow draws my affection irresistibly. I smile back. She helps me take the uncomfortably tight uniform off.

At least she's being helpful now, I tell myself. Maybe she's decided to become a more supportive friend and let me go? I'm not sure. It doesn't matter either way; I'll run out as soon as I come up with an excuse. She's too close to the boss to know why.

"If you tell me your secret," she whispers with her unmistakable, mischievous grin, "I'll tell you mine. I've never told anyone before, you know."

It occurs to me: Okay, so she really thinks I killed a whole bunch of vampires before. Fine. Now, curiosity is overcoming me and I'd like to know what her big, bad secret is. And I know the only way I can get it now: I have to stay for just a few more minutes.

"Okay, here's the truth," I begin, "I really am who you think I am, probably, but...the rumors weren't all true. Whatever it is you people all think I did in the East Coast--or in the Central Regions for that matter-- well, none of it really happened. It's all just rumors and stories."

She helps me undo my belt and asks, "Really? But I've seen you hunt already. You're a natural hunter for a girl your size. Seriously, you've got some mad talent in there."

"I guess it's my genes." I expose and gesture toward my long, sharp fangs. "Apparently, I was built to be a hunter. Maybe some people I hunted started telling stories and it blew out of proportion. I did hunt a lot in the city when I was fifteen."

She smiles. "Okay, I won't be telling anyone about your little secret then. For all they know, you really are the legendary Blonde Butcher. You sure hunt like they say you do anyway, so why not let 'em think it, right?"

"So what's your secret?" I ask with an innocent smile.

She helps me take off the uniform pants, slowly and gently. If I didn't know better, I'd say she thought I was so delicate that moving a little quicker might make my bones fall apart.

"Well, you remember that vampire you killed?" She asks.

"Yeah, what about it?"

"Well his kind is...unique."

"Yeah, I kinda noticed the scent. What's wrong

with it anyway?"

"He's a turned vampire." She smiles at me with a wink. "It was born human and it swallowed a vampire's blood."

"Wait, are you serious? You mean that's real? Did you turn that one?"

"No, no. I didn't turn it, girl. I just--"

"Oh! I get it now!" I exclaim more exuberantly than I probably should. "So that's why some of these vampires don't have the signature. I thought it was a weird regional gene pool thing."

"Shh-- Keep it down," she whispers with her hand over my mouth.

I nod.

She pushes me onto her bed playfully. I laugh out loud and feel like I'm supposed to get her back somehow, to keep the play fight going...but I don't. I just relax and go with it. Maybe she's just misguided--I'll find a way to get her to come with me to tell the others. I'm sure Thornton would give her a job too.

"So..." I try to put together all the pieces of the puzzle, "The Ruthven brothers are all turned vampires too, right?"

"Yup." She dives on top of me like a wrestler. I giggle a bit and give her a tight, loving vampire hug. She smiles like we'd just found ourselves on a whole new level of closeness.

It's alien to me, but in a good way.

"Wait," I interrupt the fun, "you said you were going to tell me something you never told anyone. But that--that's just the dead vampire's secret. And I guess the Ruthven brothers' secret. How was that *your* secret though?"

She runs her finger gently down my cheek, and continues downward. Her sharp fingernails slit my skin open around my collarbone.

It doesn't hurt. It just feels a bit cold.

She stares into my eyes with a gentle smile.

"No way," I continue, "you can't be one of them... Are you? I mean, you don't smell different. I can pick up your vampire signature from a mile away."

"No, I'm not one of them." She shakes her head and leans in to lick the blood from my collarbone. "I'm definitely not one of them." She leans in even closer and whispers directly into my ear, "I like to hunt them, girl. That's why I use the cookies. They're all suckers for my cookies. I don't know why, but it's always worked so why not use them?"

My eyes shoot open in a cold shock. "You...hunt vampires?"

"It's the flavor, Iryna. Those turned creatures are just...orgasmic."

She leans in and kisses me...on my lips.

Somehow, for a split second, I think to myself that it actually feels good. I can't deny that. I didn't expect it, and under different circumstances, I might've even given it a try. But then, my rationality takes over.

I jump up like a gunshot had gone off.

She looks disappointed, to a depth I couldn't even imagine. "What's wrong? I thought you wanted to--"

"But...you...you're a--"

"Come on. Just go ahead and say it, girl."

"Angela. You're a cannibal?!"

"Oh, that's such a nasty term." She runs her finger over my lips. "I prefer equal opportunity feeder. It sounds so much more liberal and progressive, don't you agree?"

I shove her off of me and grab my civilian clothes from the floor. "You're sick, Angela."

"You killed vampires too, right?"

"You hunted them to eat them! That's disgusting. It's your own species!" I can feel her eyes on my body so I put my clothes on as fast as vampirianly possible.

She smiles softly. "They're not really vampires, you know. Don't make such a big deal of it. They're just soulless creatures. They're mutated freaks. Niklaus Ruthven wouldn't even be alive if he wasn't already such a big man by the time I baited him."

"Wait, you baited your boss?"

She laughs aloud. "He wasn't my boss then, stupid. I was just baiting them, any of them, when he got sucked in by my bait. Those animals just can't help themselves. I damn near snapped his neck, until he told me he was the head of four of the tribes at the time. It was just four back then."

"And you ended up working for him? What's wrong with you?"

"It's just survival, girl. Niklaus offered to make me one of his top agents because, as he said, my hunting skills were so impressive and daring. So I figured, why not? I can wait till they've taken over the entire region, and then I'll just eat all the three of those guys." She winks. "Oops, I mean: They'll all just mysteriously disappear due to some unknown circumstances."

I couldn't believe my ears. "You are a disgusting vampire being, Angela. You're everything that's wrong with this world."

"Hey, it's like if we were human and we found a

cow that turned into a hybrid of it and myself--"

"Why are you still telling me all this? Aren't you afraid I would--"

She interrupts, "Would what? You think they don't know? Everyone knows what I do, girl. Everyone knows what I do and who I do. I ain't a secret. You've seen how scared they all are of me. All that matters is I've got the boss in my pocket. You ain't got nothing on me, Iryna."

A million thoughts flow through my head, all at once.

I don't know how to feel right now. It's all coming at me at the same time and none of it makes any sense. Or maybe it all makes a little too much sense for my taste. All this time, I've just been seeing what I wanted to see. Maybe it's all just confirmation bias like we talked about in class. The signs were there since the beginning and I was too stupid to acknowledge them.

The strangest part is: I have nothing at all against how she feels about me...I'm actually kind of flattered. I think a part of me would even be curious to see where things would go if I'd gone along with it and had a relationship with her.

Finding out that she likes to feed on our own kind, whether they're turned vampires or born that way, is a whole different issue. I mean, I'm open to a lot of new ideas but I've got to draw a line at cannibalism, no matter how she twists it.

Right now, I just need to get away from her. Now more than ever, I need to get to someone on the outside to help Thornton.

I dash toward the door.

Angela dashes over to me at the same speed and

slams my body against her apartment door. "You're not going anywhere, my love." She violently shoves me head to one side and sinks her fangs into my neck. It's not gentle and slow, it's brutal and it seems to crack as she bites down with the force of a predator.

She seems to drain just enough to make me weak and groggy but not enough to knock me unconscious. She knows, almost expertly, exactly when to stop--I don't even want to think about how she practiced to this point.

Yet, even now, a part of me holds onto the hope that it's all just a misunderstanding. I can't lose her. "Angela...P-- please, I just--"

"Oh, you said please?" she replies in a sarcastic tone, "then, in that case, go right ahead! Genius."

She squeezes my arm so tight it feels like it left an instant bruise. I can feel my own pulse in her grip. I can feel myself shaking in terror of the same person I would've trusted my life to just a few hours ago.

"The body of that turned creature," she says in a chilling whisper, "the one you killed. I have it stored in a safe, scent-proof, air-tight place where no one can find it. Not even you."

"Angela, I--"

She places a hand over my mouth with a gentle smile. "You will do as I say, until I say otherwise, or the entire community will know that you murdered that turned freak. And the boss won't be as merciful with you as I am. Is that understood?"

"Why? Wouldn't they all be scared of me too then? I mean, that's how you survived, right? What a legal system you have around here--they'd let me live because they'd just think I'd try to kill them all too."

"Yeah but would you? Really?"

I don't answer.

She continues, "Exactly. That's the difference between us, girl. I've proven myself. I've got the power and Ruthven's entire family knows it. He'll stop being scared of you the moment I tell him the truth about your reputation."

She throws me to the ground, away from the door, and locks it with that hollow clank. I can feel my knees and elbows crash to the floor. I'm surprised I'm still in one piece.

I couldn't believe what she's become. I look up at her with begging eyes but her eyes are nothing but aggression and arousal.

I just wish I had my friend back, the friend I thought I'd found. If only that one were real.

"Now, take your clothes off, girl." She kicks me in the side of my leg as she commands me.

"What? No!" I try to get up off the ground.

She drops her weight onto my midsection and slowly drills her fingernail toward my heart. The pain is excruciating but I try with every inch of my being to hide it and fight back. I can't.

She winks. "You're mine tonight...whether you like it or not."

I don't respond this time.

Her eyes softly glow, half closed. Her fangs are fully exposed.

She runs her hands up the side of my torso, over the wound on my ribs, and stops at my chest. She smiles like she had just fulfilled a milestone.

I close my eyes and pretend it's just a horrible nightmare...but I can't fool myself. I begin to shake even more than I did before. Tears build up under my eyes.

She slowly, deliberately, licks the side of my face and whispers, "I've wanted you since the night we met. It's too late to run now."

After an experience that I won't dignify with words, she feeds me a few drops of her blood as if it'd make it all better.

Nothing will.

CHAPTER 16

I've never felt so empty, so hollow and so cold, next to a person I once trusted. I can't stop shaking. I can't stop thinking back to what had happened with Angela. I can't quite block it all out now that I want to, and probably need to, the most. I wish I could find a way to never see her again for the rest of my life.

I never did get a chance to alert the others about Ruthven's plans--that demon girl wouldn't even let me out of her sight for one second. She used to make me feel safe. Now, I've never felt more vulnerable than I do being next to her.

We stand before a stone tower at the edge of a formerly human-run city in the North West. In the corner of my eye, I notice her tilting her head up to look at the top floors--they're surrounded by the smog. I can feel the mischievous smile on her face. I don't want to look at her right now but my eyes can't seem to block her out completely.

Even when I close my eyes, I can still see that smile. It's imprinted in me. It's a smile I used to adore with passion because I saw it on the face of my first true friend in this cold, heartless world. Today, I see that she is the cold, heartless one. I deeply, truly hate her for it.

Ivan and Donat follow closely behind us.

"This is the tower of Doctor Thornton," Ivan speaks robotically. "We will wait here."

I wonder if the man even has thoughts. I would believe it if someone told me he just had a computer program running in his brain.

"Good luck," Donat says to me with a gentle pat on my shoulder.

I flinch. "Sorry, it's not you, Donat," I whisper.

It's about six o'clock. Very few of our species have adjusted to being awake during the daylight hours so most people around here are still sound asleep.

Angela and I part ways with Ivan, who walks around to the back entrance.

Inside, Angela swiftly snaps the necks of two guards at the front door before he could even reach for an alarm button.

I feel like I'm starting to notice more about my surroundings than I usually do when I enter a new building. Maybe it's because I'm making a conscious effort to avoid all eye contact with the monster walking next to me.

On the wall, the discolored imprint of a removed corporate logo is only partly covered by a hand-written Tribal Alliance sign, haphazardly pinned up by hand. It originally said Wolfe-something. The rest of it is covered up so I couldn't tell.

Wires protrude from the walls next to the golden elevators like someone had just torn the old light fixtures off with their bare vampire fingernails.

There are boxes of candle-shaped electronic lights all around the lobby.

It reminds me of the large office buildings back in the city, except a modern vampire decorator just got his or her hands on it.

My guess is Thornton took control of this building after Ruthven started taking down the human government and corporate leaders. The doctor seems to be just as much of an opportunist as my boss is, but I still think he could be the better choice until he's done something as drastic as Ruthven already has. After all, from what I've heard so far, it sounds like Thornton's a little more into the democratic way of doing things. I'd probably vote for the man--cheers to my home city's liberal human influences.

We reach the top floor.

"You look even more pale than normal, girl," Angela dares to remark.

How dare she say that to me? I don't respond to her. I don't even turn to look at her.

Leading up to a set of shiny, black double doors is a hallway made mostly of marble. The fake-candle lights are already in place up here. I couldn't help but think that's one popular trend among West Coast vampires.

And then the seriousness of the situation sinks in: I was sent to end this great vampire leader's life. This is not something a nineteen year old girl should have to worry about, let alone have to do it together with a disgusting two-faced traitor.

On the double doors is a shiny metallic lock with a touch-screen keypad.

Angela fiddles with a pair of pliers together with

her own sharp fingernails. After a few pokes, twists and cuts, she snaps the lock open with ease. It frightens me to witness just how skilled she is at breaking into a high-end electronic lock.

As soon as we enter,

Crack!

My knee cap slams into a small wooden table right next to the door. Why would they put it there? It feels like a solid block of wood. I wince in pain.

"Shh!" Angela punches my arm.

I don't respond to her.

My heart is racing and adrenaline fills my veins. My night vision glows faintly.

I look around and see an old man in bed. It must be Doctor Thornton himself. He's sound asleep under silky, royal purple covers. I can hear his snoring... It's practically louder than the grind of a city subway train.

Angela tip-toes across the room and shifts a painting on the wall. Behind it, she picks an old-fashioned key lock with her pliers and fingernails.

Click!

The key lock opens with a louder noise than she probably expected.

The doctor's snoring seems to pause. He swallows and makes a few disgusting squishy sounds with his mouth. I freeze in terror and hope that he doesn't open his eyes.

He doesn't.

He resumes his loud snoring and Angela quietly opens the small locked panel. There's an electronic screen with security footage of...ourselves.

I wonder to myself, what is she doing? And how did she learn to do all this? I don't say any of it aloud though. I still don't want to interact with her in any way unless it's completely necessary.

Angela reaches into the electronic panel display and cuts a wire with her fingernail. The display goes blank.

She casually swings the small locked door closed and conceals it with the painting.

She grabs my arm and pulls me toward a large plate glass window right next to Thornton's bed. It lets some UV-filtered sunlight in. I couldn't help but think to myself, this man sure has a bucket's load of confidence in that smog. Even I would think twice about sleeping next to a large window like that, I don't care what's in the sky. What if the smog goes away some day? Burning to death wouldn't be fun.

"Do it, Iryna." Angela whispers. "Do it now."

I hesitate for a moment. She digs her fingernails into my arm. I pull my arm away.

Slow, quietly, I move closer to the sleeping leader and look at his peacefully dreaming face. He must be as old as the professor. He must have seen so much in his lifetime. I can't help but feel that I have no right, no right at all, to end this great elder's existence on this planet.

I begin to shake.

I can feel Angela's eyes glaring at me but I don't look at her.

Suddenly, Angela takes a violent hold of my wrist and forces my finger straight like the joint of a cat's claw. She pushes my nail toward the man's neck but, in a split second decision...I swing around and claw her in her abdomen instead.

She looks at me with fiery rage.

"Go ahead and hate me," I whisper, "but you'll die alone." I fix my eyes on her face, and if a look could kill, I'd be burning her alive from the inside out right now.

She lunges at me with quiet tip-toeing steps. I tackle her in midair, and we land on the floor next to Thornton's bed.

I swing a punch--probably the hardest punch I have ever delivered since I stopped feeding--directly onto her skull.

The sickening bone-on-bone impact sends her to the floor.

For a split second, I actually hope she's not dead. Everything in me hates her enough to want her to be, but somehow, I still don't wish it on her.

Then the urgency of the situation hits me. I quickly dash over to the sleeping doctor.

"Wake up!" I shake the old man. "Please! Wake up!"

His snore comes to a snorting, bubbling halt as he begins to swallow saliva and take in air. Slowly, he opens his eyes. He takes a moment to focus on me.

As soon as his eyes open completely, he jumps out of bed.

He moves faster than a speeding torpedo. I feel his hand grab hold of my throat. His fingers almost wrap all the way around my neck.

The next thing I know, he's got me slammed against the wall, holding my entire body up with a single arm.

"Who sent you?!" He screams at me with a frightening roar. "Answer me! Or I will snap your thin little neck like a twig!"

"P...Please...I--" I try to pull on his hands to

release the strength of his grip.

I want nothing more right now than to be able to speak to him calmly, to explain the whole situation to him, and to just help him against Ruthven.

But how can I?

What can I possibly do to make him believe that a person who just broke into his home is actually here to help him?

I close my eyes and feel tears running down my face.

"You coward...I will show no mercy." His voices thunders through my entire body.

"Adrian!" I call out with what little breath I could manage. "I...know your son...Adrian."

He loosens his grip on my throat and looks baffled. "You have five minutes to explain to me why I should not have you executed for breaking and entering into the home of the Tribal Alliance leader."

"I'm...a friend of your son's," I begin, desperately searching for the best and fastest way to explain my predicament, "We were sent here to kill you but I tried to warn your people first--"

Suddenly, Angela's hands take hold of the doctor's head. With his hand still occupied with my throat, she has a clear advantage.

Snap!

She twists his head around and smiles at me with a chilling expression of ecstasy. "Gotcha," she says to me with fangs bared.

My heart begins to race. Without a thought, I dive onto Angela and unleash a flurry of punches onto her face. Bone on bone, cracking with the sickening bruising impact of all my strength--over and over and over again.

I couldn't stop this time.

Every feeling of betrayed trust, vulnerability, fear, and hatred...released onto her head.

Suddenly, a strong hand grabs a handful of my hair and launches my entire body onto the wall.

It's Ivan with his face in a stone cold, satisfied smile. Those beady little eyes stare at me with contempt.

Finally, through his tiny little mouth, he says, "Agent Balmont, you have betrayed the United Tribes of the West Coast."

I dash toward his disproportionate body and slam him against a mirror. Pieces of mirror glass shatter onto his bald head.

He digs his fingers into my chest cavity, and shoves me away. I shoot straight upward until my spine slams onto the ceiling.

In an instant, I drop back to the floor, face first.

It jars my body from head to toe but the adrenaline has kicked in full force now--I barely feel the pain. I hop straight to my feet.

My foot meets Ivan's head. He falls backward until his skull bounces on the floor...but then he grabs my ankle, and drives a fist into my knee cap. Somehow, I ignore the pain.

I dive onto him with my fingernails aimed at his eyes...but he intercepts it with a punch that drives straight into my rib cage--right where I'd been wounded before.

Finally, I wince in pain--but only for a split second.

He tries to follow-up with another punch, but I grab onto his arm and let myself fall back...using his own weight to flip him over.

I flip myself back onto my feet, jump into the air, and pull my knee up toward my chest. As gravity pulls me back down, it helps my entire body come down as hard as vampirianly possible.

I think to myself, he's about to get the hardest stomp known to the world... straight onto his nose.

In the very last millisecond, Ivan rolls out of the way. My foot drills into the ground, and cracks the wooden flooring.

He grabs my head from behind and jabs his knee into my back. The enforcer's too fast for me.

"Goodbye," he mumbles. I could hear the smile in his voice without even looking at him.

I close my eyes and accept my fate. It's over.

Wait...the hands are gone. There's nothing, no one, holding onto me anymore. I don't seem to feel anything at all. Am I dead?

I open my eyes...and see:

Angela is grappling with Ivan, shoving each other's backs onto the walls of the room. Crash after crash, they shove each other against solid marble-looking surfaces--and neither one is willing to give up.

Suddenly, I couldn't decide how to react. I find myself stunned and confused. The pain in my knee finally takes its toll.

Slowly, I drag myself over to the solid wooden table by the door and pull myself back up to my feet. I observe the struggle by the large plate glass window.

Suddenly, I decide to do the one thing that feels like it makes sense to me.

"Hey!" I call out with my eyes locked onto them

both--fueled by all my pain and hate and feelings of helplessness from everything that had happened.

Just as both of them turn to look at me, my adrenaline-filled strength drives me to lift the solid, wooden table and hurl it toward the window. It soars through the air like a missile, launched with my arms. Even while I'm exhausted and weakened, I can throw with the power of more than three times a record-setting human weight lifter.

Ivan's beady little eyes shoot wide open. Angela dives to the ground.

The solid table nails Ivan square in the middle of his sunken chest. He falls back with a thundering crash, and flies through the large, plate glass window.

Shards of glass soar into the open sky under the UV-filtered six o'clock sun.

I hear nothing for almost ten seconds, while he remains at the mercy of the planet's gravity...until a sickening crunch on the ground below echoes through the outdoor area.

He must have fallen some fifty feet or more, I think to myself. I don't walk over to the window to look. I don't want to see it with my own eyes. It's not something I ever wanted to do to another vampire in my entire life.

I just drop to the floor, exhausted from the entire struggle. I haven't had this much activity in a single day since I stopped feeding on a regular basis. It's all finally taking its toll and at the worst possible time.

The soreness in my back and my ribs and my knee begin to swell up into a pain that feels like ten thousand metal claws.

I feel like a broken-down machine with only my very basic pieces still functioning. The air going in and out of my lungs feels dry and coarse.

I try to swallow a little saliva but my throat just seems to stick together like two pieces of sandpaper.

Angela comes closer and helps me to my feet. She strokes my hair. She offers her arm but I push it away.

She leans in to me. The warmth in her breath engulfs my face as she brings her mouth closer and closer, and whispers straight into my ear, "I saved your life because I'm not finished with you, girl."

CHAPTER 17

I weave through trunks and logs and trip over the corner of a large metal door. It was covered by tall over-grown bushes, right next to a willow tree. It's well hidden from the sight of anyone who's following the cleared pathways. I stop and carefully glance around.

Curiosity gets the better of me.

Slowly, I open the door to see what's behind it. I figure I'm leaving anyway. Why not find out before I go?

It's a dark staircase leading down into some sort of underground facility.

I hear screams and grunts coming from deep inside.

Suddenly, a man's hand lands on my shoulder. I practically jump a foot into the air.

I turn around... It's Donat.

"Don't ever creep up on me like that!" I scream and give him a friendly slap him on the chest.

"What are you doing here, Iryna?"

"I was just trying to avoid running into Angela but

I ended up stumbling onto this door, so I..."

"Join me. We need all the help we can get, beautiful." He leads me down the staircase into the underground level.

"What is this place?" I look around and see an endless sea of injured vampires.

"This is my top secret First Aid facility for the United Tribes' Regional Army," he answers. "Niklaus refuses to provide funding for the wounded so I am running this with what limited resources I have access to."

As we walk through the facility, I notice that the injured aren't on anything resembling hospital beds. They're just lying on the cold, dirt-covered floors. Some of them have thin blankets under them but not everyone even has that much. A lot of them have missing limbs, severe lacerations, and a few are even burnt.

"What happened to them all?"

Donat stops and turns to face me. "It is a disaster, Iryna. When my brother ordered the invasion of the major cities, his forces were given instructions to attack and kill all of the humans who administered the governments and the communications networks. In theory, Niklaus believed that he would sever their ability to call for help and dethrone their rulers. But when the human national leaders learned of the casualty rates, they immediately knew that they could not fight my brother's forces with traditional methods. The few survivors of their human staff informed their leaders of the nature of the attackers. Our forces were described as fierce, immortal creatures from hell. In fear, ignorance, and desperation, they ordered attacks on the entire occupied cities with bombs and other aerial weapons."

"The professor was afraid something like that might happen, but I never thought they'd go that far..."

"Fear is a strong motivation for us all, Iryna. Ignorance amplifies its damage. They felt they could sacrifice the few survivors in exchange for the protection of their remaining cities."

"So it's turned into a war?"

"There is no war. The human national leaders engaged in an exchange of bombings with their peers from overseas. Their entire governing system has been destroyed. The few surviving members of the human species are dying from the respiratory illnesses."

"So... the East Coast is all...gone?"

"No, Iryna, only the humans who had remained on the surface. Based on our latest communications with the East Coast tribes, their vampire population took necessary precautions long before the region was attacked by the overseas humans. Their end of the continent is almost entirely populated by our species now--with the exception of the local vampire families' human farms."

I nod. "So the professor was right. We aren't ready. It's all going to hell now."

"Yes, Marsden was right. In time, the blanket in the sky would have prompted many of our kind to take control of the human cities, in a peaceful manner. Gradually, through the established channels, our people would have taken over the workforce and the leaderships of the nations and the corporations. Instead, Niklaus chose force and impatience. He is a showman, and a charismatic man of deception. He cannot lead us into a peaceful, constructive future. We must find a better solution."

"So why didn't you just take over since the start?"

Donat points to his own face. "Look at me, Iryna. The tribe leaders, of any region, would never support a man with this face as its governing leader. I am not delusional. I know it is the way of the world we live in."

"I get it... We really haven't come a long way, have we?"

"No, I understand my place in this world. You, on the other hand would make an excellent leader..."

"Oh, no," I interrupt. "There's no way I'm going into politics. I'd die if I knew I was responsible for something like this."

"But you would not be. As a regional government, we must be led by one with intelligence and empathy. You would be an excellent candidate."

I shudder. "You're thinking way too highly of me, Donat. I'm not that perfect."

"Regardless, Niklaus must be replaced. He cannot remain leader of this region, or any territory for that matter."

"I agree with you... But what are we gonna do? Wars only kill and injure more of our own people. Look at the humans. We can't all keep repeating the same mistakes. The world's soap opera needs to end... We all need to learn."

He smiles. "For now, we must simply help those who are in need... and those who have been hurt by my brother's reckless tactics. In time, we will find a way to remove him from power... when the opportunity presents itself."

I look around at all the wounded.

I want to help them all but the few of us can only do so much at once. I'm beginning to understand a little better how it felt in all those situations that I'd only read about in books.

I notice a young red-haired girl... It's Bubble. She has a severely burnt leg and it's not even bandaged. She's screaming in agony.

After everything that's happened, I figure it's time to put aside our little childish and petty differences. It's time to find out what her real name is.

"Let me help this one first," I tell Donat and gesture toward the girl.

"That one cannot be helped, Iryna. We do not have any anesthetics or--"

"It's okay, Donat. I know what to do." I smile with a pat of reassurance.

He nods. "You are a very kind and gentle vampire being."

I approach Bubble with a gentle smile and drop to my knees next to her. "Hey, let me take a look at that."

She continues to wince in pain, but her screams die down. "Hey, you're...the new girl, right? I'm really, really sorry. I wasn't always such a--"

"Don't worry. I'm here to help you." I hold out my arm right in front of her fangs.

She manages a little laugh. "I'm burnt, not starving...but thanks for trying."

"Okay then..." I run a sharpened fingernail down my palm and let a few drops of my blood drip onto her injured leg.

"Is... is that going to work?" She looks scared more

than anything now.

"I tried it on my ex before and it worked wonders," I reply quietly. "Maybe I've got special genes or something. From what I remember, it dulls the pain a bit so it's the next best thing when they're out of painkillers."

After a minute, she calms down and smiles.

I move in closer to her. "My name's Iryna, by the way... What's your name?"

"I'm Sara," she manages to answer while she takes a deep breath, "and I'm a big dumb stupid head."

I chuckle at her cutesy, childish choice of words. No wonder she never spoke much. "Why would you say a thing like that?"

She slows her breathing more. "Jamie wasn't always like that, you know."

"Who's Jamie?"

"The tall, bleached blonde one that hurt you?" She answers as if she's asking the question. After a pause, she leans back and looks up. "When I first moved here, she was like the nicest person ever. But after Angela attacked her, she hasn't been the same since. I tried to help her but--"

"Oh, I didn't know..."

"I know Angela's your friend and all, but she--"

"She's not really my friend... Not anymore."

Sara looks away. "I'm going to miss Jamie so much. I can't even imagine living a day without her and now, I--"

"Wait. She's dead? What happened?" I couldn't believe my ears. Somehow, it never even crossed my mind that she could be dead. We always take the people we meet in person for granted--as if they could never die the way others, the ones we only

THE DESCENDANTS: DAWN OF THE VAMPIRE AGE

hear about from a distance, always could.

"Yeah...we were drafted. I thought you knew. We ended up in the same unit too; we thought we were so lucky... When they stationed us in the South-West, we loved it at first--we always wanted to visit there eventually so it was like a dream come true. But then they sent her into some T.V. building to kill the humans that ran the place, and like five minutes later, the human government's airplanes dropped some big bullet-looking thing on it and..." Tears begin to roll down her cheeks. "I tried to save her... I really tried-- but I couldn't. It was too late. I should've been faster!"

"You survived." I try to comfort her with the only upside I could think of.

"No. I wish I didn't. I really wish I didn't. It was my fault. I hesitated...I was scared. And I shouldn't have been. They trained me and I was still scared, and that was my friend in there!"

I place a hand on her shoulder. "I'm so sorry."

I couldn't help but feel a deep sense of guilt for acting the way I did to Jamie the last time I saw her alive. I know she was an alpha bitch and probably deserved to get her ass kicked, but she definitely didn't deserve to die--certainly not for the ambitions of Niklaus Ruthven, or the fear and paranoia of the humans. I just wish I'd bothered to find out her name before she died. The last thing I said to her was that I really didn't care what her name was--I'll never be able to fix that now.

I notice a family surrounding an injured male a few feet away from us.

"Hey, do you have any family around here?" I ask Sara.

"Not around here... My parents hate me now. They hate everything about me. My friends back home told me the rumors, about how there's the United Tribes out here, and how great it all was... so I picked up and came as fast as I could. Now look at me five years later. I'm so stupid."

"It's not your fault... Why do you think your parents hate you?"

She pulls in a deep breath. "Because they do, okay? They really do. They don't like anything I ever do... Like when they built a farm before I left, they said they worked so hard to grow healthy prey, 'cause of all the diseases or something. They thought I'd be all happy and start a family there... But that's just not me. I think it's disgusting feeding on humans like the elders."

"...You don't feed either?" I glance at her body. She's thinner than I am, as far as I can tell.

"Well, not on meats. It's gross. Even the humans and other mammals have vegetarians, right? So me and a few of my friends back home...we developed these healthy substitute things. It doesn't taste that good yet, but--"

"Wait. You're a...umm--"

"Yeah, I'm a B.E.T.H." She smiles. "It's okay to say it. My friends changed it to Bitches for the Ethical Treatment of Humans. We're proud of it. It's not even just for the humans though, it's healthier for us too. We found new ways to extract nutrients from stuff like nuts and vegetables...like without needing a human stomachs and livers to filter it for us and mix into their blood stream first. It keeps us alive and healthier too."

I gently pat her on her head, surprised I'd

completely misjudged her. She has a child-like innocence about her that makes her irresistibly adorable.

She stares at me for a moment. "So do you feed on alternatives too?"

"No... Why?"

"Oh, I just wondered... You're so skinny. I just thought, maybe you did 'cause no one can stay thin feeding on those fatty, carby, junk-food-guzzling humans these days, and-- Well, I should shut up. You're probably just lucky with the genes then."

"No. I just don't feed at all." I shrug.

"Oh...no, no, you shouldn't do that, *Iry*. There's healthier ways to keep your weight down. What good is looking hot if you can't live centuries and centuries to enjoy it?"

For a second, I hesitate to correct her... "Umm, it's Iryna. My name's Iryna."

"You gave me some of your blood, and you helped me, so now I want to help you too. And I think that kind of makes us friends now, right? So can I just call you Iry from now on?"

I shrug. "You are one strange little girl...and I mean that in a good way."

"No, I get it." And then her sad puppy eyes get me.

"Yeah. You can call me Iry if you want."

"Okay." She looks happier than a person should be for such a small favor. "Hey, I think your blood's really working. It doesn't hurt so much anymore."

"So where were you from originally?" I ask.

"A small town in the East Coast, just north of the city...it's a long way from here. Like I said, I'm really stupid for coming here."

"Really? I'm from the East Coast too. I lived in the

city for most of my life though."

"Oh!" She hesitates with eyes wide open. "I'm so sorry, I didn't mean to imply that you're stupid... I mean you're obviously not stupid. In fact, I think you're very, very--"

"Relax. It's okay." I pat her and smirk. "And hey, what do you mean I'm skinnier than you? You're like the tiniest thing I've seen on this side of the continent." I nudge her with a smirk.

She laughs--it's a bit squeaky and high pitched but, under the circumstances, I'd feel guilty for being annoyed by her. "Have you seen yourself in a mirror before, Iry?"

"Hey, they say I'm a pretty fierce hunter." I wink.

The laughter disappears from her face. "Hey, wait a minute. You're not the Blonde Butcher, are you?"

Now, I think she's half serious. "Umm, no... What's with that anyway? Sir Ruthven said something about that."

Suddenly, Sara's smile disappears. "You don't know the legend of the Blonde Butcher?"

"I didn't grow up in a small town with a vampire family. In the city, all I ever heard were human news and rumors, so--"

"Well, legend has it...the Blonde Butcher is this skinny little blonde girl from the East Coast who murdered her entire family in cold blood. She was just a little kid at the time. I thought it was just an urban vampire legend, but lately, I heard down the grapevine Ruthven got her to join some special secret forces thing. It's probably all just stories to scare people. People like to make things up."

My heart skips a beat. "She murdered her whole family?"

"Yeah. They say she picked up and moved to the Central regions first... She slaughtered, like, families and families of humans and tore out their hearts...but she never fed on them. She just did it for sport--for fun. That's all she did for years and years. By the time she was like seventeen, the tribes in the Central regions got worried. It was getting bad. So they sent her a message: stop killing our food for sport, or we'll hunt you down."

"So that's when she stopped?"

"No, she just got mad. She asked around, she talked to all the vampires on the streets, just to find out which tribe was the biggest, baddest, most powerful one of them all. And then, according to the legends, she hunted down each and every member of that tribe, and murdered them in cold blood. And she tore out their hearts too, just like she did to the humans. It's like her signature."

My face gets even paler than it usually is.

Donat taps me on the shoulder. I jump. Sara laughs at me with a lovable smile.

"I apologize for the interruption, Iryna," Donat whispers quietly. "But there is a large, injured man on the south wing who is lashing out against our workers. We need all the assistance we can get in restraining him."

"Okay, no problem." I hop up to my feet.

Sara grabs my hand. "Hey, Iry...if you ever need help with anything, anything at all, I owe you now. I can even teach you about healthy vampire nutrition stuff, if you want. You can stay skinny and be a lot healthier."

I nod and smile before walking away. She's a beautiful little person inside and out, and if I hadn't given her a chance beyond my first impression of her, I wouldn't have even bothered to find out her real name. Well she's definitely not Bubble to me anymore... she's not even as dumb as I thought she was. She's one of my only friends now. She's Sara.

Half way to the opposite end of the facility, Donat whispers to me, "How did you do that, Iryna?"

"How'd I do what?"

"How did you stop the girl's pain? We are in a deep shortage of pain medications yet your technique seems to be more effective than most of our supplies."

"Placebo goes a long way when there's no other choice."

He pats me on the back. "As I said, you would make a wonderful leader someday...if only you would allow yourself to be."

CHAPTER 18

Professor Marsden stands in the middle of the class circle and begins her lecture. At this point, Sir Niklaus Ruthven has gained complete and unopposed control of the West Coast region so class attendance is getting back to normal. That is, except for one student: I don't see Adrian anywhere in sight. And I don't blame him after what had happened to his father. I wouldn't be here today either, if I were in his shoes.

Angela sits three students down from me. It wasn't her choice--she's flustered. I just timed my arrival carefully to avoid sitting next to her today. She probably isn't surprised anyway, but by the look on her face, she's probably trying to come up with a way to follow me after class.

She listens to the professor speak, staring blankly with the bruises on her face shamelessly displayed. She seems to be as numb to the situation as I felt when I walked with her into the tower. Well, maybe not that numb. If she's looking for sympathy, she can go crawl somewhere else for it.

After class, I run up to Professor Marsden. "May I help out in your research lab after class...if you don't mind? Please?"

She looks at me and locks onto my eyes.

"Sure you may, dear," she answers with a smile.

"Can I come too, professor?" Angela jumps in and asks the professor.

I don't look at Angela at all.

I just focus on the professor's eyes and hope she can somehow hear my thoughts. I know she was probably being sarcastic about the whole psychic thing... but right now, I hope she really can hear my pleas.

"I am very sorry, darling," the professor tells Angela with a forced smile, "it is a very small laboratory and I can only allow one student at a time."

I try not to show my reaction but I'm smiling from ear to ear on the inside. Maybe she really heard me, or maybe she picked up on what I was pleading for in my mind. Either way, I owe her.

Professor Marsden's lab is an underground sphere with walls that seem to be made entirely of solid metal plates, painted white. It's not as small as she made it sound.

The professor slouches over a blood sample on a cold, metal table. She squints at it.

"By the way...thank you so much, professor," I finally tell her, "for letting me come here, I mean."

"I know and see far more than you credit me for," she replies without taking her eyes away from her research. "It is a side effect of my many centuries of experience."

"Speaking of knowing things, did you already know who I was before you met me?"

"No, dear." She looks up at me. "Why do you ask such a strange question?"

"I mean like did you track me down, because of some rumors you'd heard about a... hunter?"

She laughs loudly. "Heavens, no. I had never even known of your existence before the moment we met in the city."

"Oh, I thought maybe Ruthven got you to track me down and--"

She laughs again. "I certainly would not have aided that con-man in his political scheme. You should remember the reason why."

I pause for a moment. "I...should?"

"Iryna, my observant darling, Niklaus Ruthven is the fraudulent 'psychic' con man I had encountered forty years ago. It was me who turned him into one of our species--though not purposely, of course."

"Oh!" I feel like an idiot. "Wait, so you turned him?"

She explains, "Yes... It did not surprise me when such a charismatic and deceiving man chose to become a politician. What surprised me was when he had resurfaced forty years later with the same appearance, as one of our own. He even adopted the name of a mythological symbol. To his credit, he ceased to continue his psychic business after our encounter."

"But how'd you turn him?"

"Remember the blood I had fed to him? As it turns out, my blood had gradually transformed his biology through a mechanism that even I was unaware of after centuries. It was simply not a scenario that I anyone I met had thought to test purposely, let alone in a controlled setting."

"So you accidentally turned him when you just wanted to trick him into thinking you could track his movements?"

"Yes, dear. And he charismatically united ten of the tribes in this region and, as recent generations say, the rest is history. For that, I blame myself..."

"Well, it's not your fault... You didn't even know."

"On the bright side, however, he was the very reason I had begun to research the turning of humans. It was a major discovery for our scientific community."

I browse around in the lab to calm my nerves.

There are charts all over the wall. I have no idea what any of them mean. I see a whole library of binders. Maybe she likes to keep her research in hard copy form. It just amazes me the kind of information she must have in here.

"I didn't know we could turn them till... someone told me about him," I add.

"That is because our scientific journals do not reach the city and, I trust, the human-owned libraries you frequented do not carry vampirian literature," she replies with a chuckle. "It's quite an interesting phenomenon, really. No other species, to our knowledge, has ever had the ability to transform an evolutionary predecessor into its own species through blood ingestion."

"I always thought it was just a human myth."

"As did I, and most of our species. After extensive research, I have determined that there is a forty nine percent chance of turning a human into a fellow vampire, if it ingests any amount of our blood."

"What happens to the rest?"

"The rest, it appears, suffers extreme disfiguration at best."

"At best? I'm afraid to ask what the worst case scenario is."

"Death, my dear. In fact, it causes the most unlucky of them to melt into a pile of flesh and blood on the floor, not unlike the portrayal of our deaths in many human works of fiction."

I cringe. "Sounds pretty. So I take it Sir Ruthven's brothers were some of the unlucky disfigured ones?"

"Ivan became mildly disfigured when Niklaus decided that he wanted his brother to survive as his enforcer... to help in his political agenda."

"And he still decided to go ahead and turn his other brother?"

"No. Donat is not his brother in the biological sense. Donat is, in truth, centuries his senior. He began using the title of brother after he met Niklaus about fifteen years ago. They claimed to be brothers to avoid suspicion in the human cities and they have grown accustomed to the title since then."

"But Donat really is related to him, right? So how'd he get turned?"

The professor nods. "In his youth, Donat was uncontrollably attracted to vampire females--he still is, at times. He surrounded himself with every vampire female he met. Eventually, he allowed one of them to feed on him for pleasure, but without killing him. In the process, his friend had accidentally lacerated her own lips, and so he ingested her blood. It was not on purpose."

"I've heard a story like that...well, in a different situation. I never thought it was real though. But wow...he really tells you everything, doesn't he?"

"As I said, Iryna... Donat is a trusted friend. He is involved in Niklaus' political agenda by relation but not by choice. Niklaus Ruthven is a persuasive man in many ways."

"Well they're lucky neither of them died like some of the other fifty-one percent, I guess."

"The most fascinating aspect of a turned vampire is their undying craving for simple carbohydrates... Sugars and starches."

"...Like cookies?"

"Yes... They crave all forms of solid foods that are easily digestible such as simple sugars, especially when blended with human blood. It appears the mutation in their metabolic process causes a Ketogenic condition similar to humans on a low-carbohydrate diet--along with all its cravings. It remains to be seen if their average life span will be shortened by their condition, however."

"You think they may not live as long as we do?"

"They will survive far longer than a human, for sure. However, I suspect that there will be an increased risk of insulin-related health problems, especially for those who regularly succumb to their simple carbohydrate cravings."

"So...Do you know anyone else around here that was turned?"

Adrian enters the lab.

I didn't even notice him come in. I guess he already knows the entry code. He didn't even have to knock.

"My dear Adrian..." The professor looks up from

her work. "My deepest condolences. Your father was a great leader and he will be missed."

"Thanks," he replies.

I feel like I should say something too but I just freeze. I feel partly responsible for his loss and probably shouldn't look at him right now.

He glances at me and doesn't say a word. He looks a little surprised to see me here though.

"Should I leave?" I whisper to the professor.

"No, dear," she answers with a light pat on my shoulder and a wink. "The two of you should get to know each other."

"But professor," I whisper as softly as vampirianly possible, "didn't you say only one student was allowed in here at a time?"

"As I said before...I know and see far more than you credit me for, dear." She nudges me. "Plus, Adrian has been my research assistant for some time. He does not count toward the quota."

After a minute or two, the professor conveniently leaves the room. Stupid-me finally catches on.

Adrian and I sit in complete silence for what feels like a full minute. I'm having the most awkward moment since the last time I tried to date a fellow vampire in the city.

The help of an elder in a potential dating situation is the worst thing to add to the awkwardness of a first conversation.

And then it finally hits me. That shouldn't even be the first thing on my mind right now.

"I'm so sorry for your loss," I finally speak out.

"I always thought it was weird how people say that," he replies with a shrug. "I mean like, why are you sorry? You had nothing to do with it. So don't

ARIES BRAEBURN

be."

Another moment of awkward silence assaults the flow of our conversation. Somehow, I finally notice that he seems to be staring at my eyes--constantly. That's weird...

He adds, "Sorry, I didn't mean to sound rude. What I should've said is... Thank you. You seem like a really nice girl."

I'm surprised he seems as nervous as I am.

"Hey, you know anything about Scarbromine?" I ask with a stupid half-smile. In my mind, I smack myself upside the head. All I could think of to talk about was a drug? What's wrong with me?

He just laughs, "Is that a trick question? I thought you already knew a little too much about it."

"Huh? What do you mean?"

"Oh, nothing... It's just that I heard your best friend just loaded up on, like, enough of the crap to knock out a horse."

"Wait, you mean Angela? She bought Scarbromine?"

"Yeah, I thought she loaded up on it to party with you. She's like the only one you hang out with, right?"

"I don't know what she's up to but that's definitely not for me. We're not really talking anymore so--"

He shrugs. "It's okay. I don't do it anymore but it's not like I'd report you or anything if you do."

I try to change the subject to something he's probably dying to talk about. "So what do you really think caused the smog? The humans? Our government?"

"My theory is...that jackass Niklaus Ruthven's been in cahoots with hundreds of human corporations since day one. Either he snuck some custom formulated gas into their factory emissions or he's been contributing to it using his own exhaust systems. It's obvious he's responsible though, if you ask me."

I chuckle at the elaborate theory. "I haven't heard that one before."

"Yeah, I'm just a conspiracy nut behind it all."

"Oh, sorry... I didn't mean to laugh. Go on."

"Okay, well, just think: Why didn't it happen before, a hundred years ago when the human corporations were even more careless with the environment? No, Ruthven needed a catalyst to launch his campaign, and he needed a reason to take over the region--at the expense of millions of lives. When they start telling the public things that don't quite make sense, it's always some secret agenda behind it all, if you ask me. The truth makes sense but lies always have more holes than Swiss cheese."

I smile brightly. "Well sometimes simplifying makes you miss things too...but, no, that's the smartest thing I've ever heard." In my mind, I'm thinking that's just the smartest thing I've heard coming out of his mouth. But, sometimes, leaving out a few words makes it a little nicer coming out. Cheers to my social skill development!

"Don't you and Angela still work for Ruthven? I thought you'd argue with me more over all this, to be honest."

"No, I'm really not friends with her anymore. And I just sort of stumbled into everything... I never really believed any of the manipulative stuff that Ruthven said to us. The professor told me about his past anyway... I don't put blind trust in people who try to use and take advantage of everyone."

He winks. "Then I like you already."

I just stare blankly for a moment like someone had just handed me a winning lottery ticket. I try to cover up my reaction. I mean, he probably didn't mean it the way I'd wanted him to mean it anyway.

He just smiles afterward. I hope it's in a good way.

Well, whether he meant it that way or not, I never thought any of this would ever happen. We actually agree on our world views in some ways.

I'm just surprised I could actually talk to Adrian at this point. I didn't even expect to be able to look him in the eyes after everything that happened.

Afterwards, we take a walk outside, in the forest area surrounding the underground lab.

"I wasn't sure I should say this, but...your father probably would've been a better leader than Ruthven. I would've supported him."

He nods. "Thanks, I appreciate that. Really."

"Hey, you know...you could probably take over someday. After all, you've got his genes in you--"

"Actually, I--"

"Oh, did I say something wrong again? Sorry, I'm so stupid--"

"No, it's not you. I just don't usually tell people this but I was adopted so...there's no shared genes in the Thornton's. It was just a name we used for the human governments to keep track of us."

"Sorry." I look down and wish for a rewind.

"Hey, I didn't know we had so much in common," he interrupts the awkwardness. "I thought you were with Angela."

"I already said, we aren't friends anymore so--"

"No, I mean, you know, with... Sorry, I shouldn't have said anything. I'm offending you."

"Oh!" My eyes shoot wide open, both literally and figuratively. "No, no, it's okay. You can say it. But no, I never really was--at least I never knew I was." I'd add that I may not have minded it up until a certain point, but again, I know where to end my sentences now...sometimes.

"It's just that I saw the way she looked at you and the way you smiled at each other. And everyone's seen how she was with every other girl she liked, so I just thought--"

"Okay, I get it, Adrian."

"I just thought you knew..."

"No, I didn't know about the others but I guess it needed to be said. I always see what I want to see. It just makes me blind to everything that's ready to hurt me and everyone around me."

He pauses and seems to be reconsidering something. "Okay... Well this is when I'd tell you we could, like, hang out after class sometime, but..."

My head drops. "It's okay. You don't have to explain."

He ducks down with a smile and tries to catch my gaze again. "No, I meant I'm heading to the East Coast with the others so I can't stay."

"Oh. You're leaving?"

"It's not just me. Over the next few months, everyone around here that doesn't agree with Ruthven's administration will be heading east. We're going to form a new Tribal Alliance with the locals, in honor of Doctor Thornton. The first group of us is gonna be leaving tomorrow. I can bring you with me, if you want. My friend had to cancel so I've got an extra ticket."

My eyes light up. "Are you serious?"

"Well, you don't have to. I just figured, if you're not tied down or anything here, you might like it a bit better over there. You'd fit in with us."

"Yeah!" I answer, in a much higher volume than I mean to. "I mean... Yeah, I'd love to come."

A smile bursts out of my face and I have to use every bit of strength in me to hold back my internal fireworks celebration. I don't want to seem overly excited and scare him away at this point.

He seems to get it. He smiles and adds, "Okay, meet us by the train station tomorrow morning. The train leaves at eleven o'clock A.M.--we had to make it late so most of the community would be asleep when we sneak out. Try not to fall asleep or anything, okay?"

I nod with a nervous smile. "I won't."

I imagine us tilting our heads at the same time, and moving closer and closer...until we sink our fangs into each other and share a love loop until the end of time.

But we don't. I just stand awkwardly with my eyes fixed on him as he smiles and turns to walk away.

After we part ways, I still jump around like a caffeinated bunny for a few minutes. I'm glad no one's around to see it.

I can't quite picture myself in anything good right now but I also never thought I'd leave the East Coast in the first place, let alone be able to talk to Adrian. So who am I to say what my crazy future self will, or will not, decide to do?

After everything that's happened with Niklaus Ruthven as my boss, it's time to get away from all this and start fresh.

For a moment, I stand alone in silence and just smile to myself like a little child who found an early Christmas present. My excitement is swallowing my entire body. My heart literally feels like it's sinking into my chest--but in a good way, this time.

There's only one thing on my mind now: Time needs to move faster!

Suddenly, I feel a sharp pain on the side of my neck that feels all too familiar.

The world fades away from me.

My eyes feel heavy and my limbs tingle and I lose sense of my surroundings. My senses tell me nothing...but the smell of horse radish.

CHAPTER 19

In the hallway of the house I had dreamt of before, the entire dream of the blue-eyed girl repeats itself, step by step.

The blue-eyed girl stands frozen and smiles with her hands covered in fresh blood. I walk toward the large door at the end of the hallway where a pool of crimson liquid is spreading...

This time, I don't wake up. I can't.

Instead, I see two adults spread out over the floor of what looks to be the master bedroom. I think to myself, Why don't I remember this? Is it even real?

A stocky man who looks glossy enough to be a few centuries old--lies cold under the window of the room. His body looks to be gray and hard, frozen rock solid, with his green eyes wide open in a state of eternal shock.

The other is a blonde woman of around the same age with her face permanently paused on a silent scream.

I move in closer.

The chest cavities appear shredded and brutally

drilled-through. It's not machine-like. It's raw and animal-like--more so than any civilized vampire would even do to the prey, let alone our own kind.

"I had to end it tonight," the blue-eyed girl whispers. "They hurt us every night...and it had to be stopped. I'm setting you free now, baby girl."

She reaches toward me and I feel another sharp pain in my neck. The distinct scent of horse radish assaults my nasal passages again.

"I have to go now," she continues. "I'll always love you."

"Valeska!" I try to call out. "Please don't go!" But the words only seem to ring through my mind. I can't move my mouth...and she doesn't hear me.

My eye lids feel heavy again and my limbs are tingling. This time, the feeling gets deeper and deeper until my entire body feels numb and my vision fades to white. I feel the distinct sensation of falling down, like I'm being pulled into an endless pit of emptiness.

An infinite void.

Cold, hard reality reappears. I wouldn't say it's better than where I'd just come from.

I look down and see that I'm nineteen again and lying flat on the floor of Angela's apartment. I can feel her around me...literally.

It's worse.

Angela is straddling my body with her strong legs wrapped around my waist. She feels warm, but it's not a comforting kind of warm--more like a burn-me-alive kind of warm. My wrists and ankles are tied down to her bed. I'm not wearing any clothes... I'm just in my underwear. And as thankful as I am, I'm surprised she even left that on.

"Angela--"

She fires off her mischievous smile. "I told you I wasn't finished with you. Where'd you try to run?"

She takes a deep breath. It looks like she's gathering her thoughts. Finally, she smiles and leans in toward my face. She lightly scratches the skin over my heart.

I try as hard as I can to not show the pain and I'm almost succeeding this time. I've had more practice lately than a person should in an eternity.

"Shh... Relax, my beautiful little angel girl." She breathes on my face and it smells like death.

"Could you, please, just untie me?"

"When I'm feeling like it." She runs her sharpened fingernails slowly toward my eye. I flinch. She whispers, "Does that hurt?"

I feel a sharp pain on my cheek. It gets even worse. "Angela, please... just..."

"It's too late for that now, girl. I told you not to talk to that Adrian boy. Now look what you've made me do."

She rolls her knuckles over my heart, back and forth. With her other hand, she slowly re-opens the wound on my ribs. I couldn't help but suspect she's the one Jamie copied that from.

I can tell by her sadistic grin that she's enjoying it now more than ever.

The pain gets deeper. It's crossing my threshold. My heart begins to race. My mind begins to panic. I lose sight of where I am and who I'm with.

No! Fight her, I tell myself. I'm a hunter, I'm a survivor. I can get through this. I will. I can. There must be a way.

Suddenly, I open my eyes and stare directly into Angela's with a seductive grin on my face. Well, I try to make it as seductive as I can but it might look awkward right now.

She looks utterly confused.

I slow my breathing and force myself to relax my nerves as much as possible. It numbs the pain just a bit.

"Do you have any idea how long I've waited to have you on me like this?" I ask her with a low, soft, tone. "The first day we met, the first time I saw your eyes, I knew you were the one for me. You were the one I wanted. We need each other, Angela."

I slowly lick my lips and try my very best to keep it subtle and real. I don't want to cross into caricature territory.

Slowly, hesitantly, she takes her hands away from my heart and my wound. I can feel my blood drip down the side of my body. I don't care. There are bigger, more threatening things on me right now than a little blood loss.

In my mind, I force myself to believe all the words I just said. I'll lie to myself and convince myself enough to make it feel real for a few minutes.

I see the expression on her face subtly change. Tiny little cues in her eyes signal that she's beginning to believe it. I guess a part of her wants to, even longs to, believe it's all real.

It's her wildest dreams come true and she couldn't resist the temptation of letting herself fall for it. Just the tiniest little possibility that maybe, just maybe, it's real...seems to be enough to make it worth her while to believe it. It's a technique used for greed and selfish purposes all the time--it's time someone put it to good use.

"Untie me," I venture to add. "Let me feel your soft, smooth skin in my hands."

She hesitates for a moment. I can just picture the confusion and desire, fear and raging hormones, all mixing it up in her head right about now.

"It's okay, Angela, my love," I smile at her with my eyes focused deep into hers, convincing myself as much as I could that she is beautiful and perfect to me. "You can trust me. This is everything I ever wanted. I want to spend the rest of my life with you. It's us against the world, right?" My eyes begin to tear up a little.

She wipes the blood from my ribs and kisses it. I wince in pain...and quickly turn it into an expression of pure pleasure.

I lick my lips again and pretend to enjoy it. I let the feeling sink in to my very being, to make it look as real as I possibly can.

Slowly, she unties my wrists and my ankles, careful to hold me down just enough so I couldn't escape right away. She keeps all her weight on my waist but I'm not even trying to escape--not yet anyway. I know exactly what she's thinking.

Over the next half hour, I make the ultimate personal sacrifice in order to gain my freedom.

I will never forgive myself for many of the things I've done in my life, but never before have I felt so much like I'm about to bathe with pure bacteria in a dumpster on a humid day.

Afterward, Angela smiles at me.

I can see it in her half-closed eyes: She's released her pressure and seems to trust me again.

She sits at the edge of the bed. "I'm so sorry. I never wanted to hurt you, girl," she says. "I thought you never liked me."

I pat her gently and stay down on her bed. Sometimes, the most logical thing to do isn't the most effective. I've hunted enough in my early teens to know that there are times when you need to act, and there are times when you should sit tight to get your target.

Right now, I'm sitting tight.

She talks for a few minutes. I don't hear a word she says; I'm running all the possible scenarios through my mind. I'm trying to think of every way she could react to everything I could possibly do from this point forward. I need to be ready. Now, it's life or death, and it's time to discover who I truly am when push comes to shove.

She gets up to her feet. "I'm gonna take a shower, okay? I trust you... If you're still here when I come out, I'm going to be the happiest vampire in the world. If not, then...well, you're free to go. It's your choice."

I smile at her but I don't believe her for one second. "Okay. I'm not going anywhere," I tell her softly.

Deep down, I want to cry my eyes out. I wish I could believe her love was all real but I'm not that stupid. I know her ties to Niklaus Ruthven and I know how she would really react if I leave. I won't make it fifty feet away from this apartment complex before she'd have a squad of Ruthven's secret service take me into custody.

While Angela takes a shower, I realize that there's only one thing I can do. I have to defend myself, not physically but mentally. And if I fail, then no one gets hurt but me. I'm used to that risk.

I run over to her fridge and search through it on the odd chance she was stupid enough to leave the pieces of the dead vampire in here. Maybe she lied about where she'd hidden it.

...Well, apparently not.

There's no trace of the evidence in her fridge.

I hear her shower turn off. I need to hurry one way or the other: out or back to bed. Either way, I've got to move as fast as I--

Crash!

In my desperate scramble, my foot knocks over the tall garbage can next to her fridge.

What the hell? That's just weird, I think to myself. That wasn't there before. Why would she move it to some random place, right in front of the fridge?

And then the answer comes. In fact, the answer falls all over the floor as the garbage can drops and opens.

Bones, all licked clean of flesh, scatter across the

floor of Angela's apartment kitchen like some human spare rib restaurant's dumpster just tipped over.

Aside from the scent of Angela's saliva, I recognize a trace of something else: It's the scent of the dead vampire I had hunted. I will never forget it for as long as I breathe.

She lied!

She didn't stash it in some secret location. She has it right here in her kitchen--well, technically, she had most of it in her digestive tract.

Either way, she doesn't have anything to blackmail me with anymore and she's just taking advantage of the opportunity now.

Still, I need to keep up appearances for the time being. It's all happening too fast and I can't think straight. I just know I shouldn't burn the bridge just yet. I'm not ready...my plan isn't ready.

I scramble to pick up all the bits and pieces of the vampire carcass and toss it back into the garbage can. I move faster than I ever have in my life.

Angela comes out of the bathroom, in a robe...

I literally landed on her bed a split second before she opens the bathroom door.

She looks around the room and pauses. She focuses on me with a neutral expression. Then, she finally says, "You just made me the happiest woman in the world, girl."

I look at her and smile, innocently. She smiles back. I'm home free.

"Let me give you a back rub, girl," she says with a gentle smile. I hesitate. She adds, "You won't believe how good it feels. Everyone tells me I give the best back rubs in the entire region...honestly."

I slowly lie face down on her bed, and look up at the wall ahead. She begins her routine with gentle circles, pressing a little harder as she moves toward my shoulder blades.

She presses her entire weight on the small of my back. It stings a bit, but that's the least of my problems right now. She's got me held down. All I need is to convince her it's all okay and I can find a way out of this mess, calmly. I'll find a way to give her what she really deserves before I leave.

I'm almost at the finish line now. "Angela. Wanna come with me to the--"

Suddenly, I notice there's one piece of carcass left and it's in the open! It was so small, I didn't even notice.

She presses on my back and leans in close to my ear. "So, what were you looking for, my love?" She asks in a whisper.

"I... I just wanted to see if--"

She presses a little harder. "Now, before you answer, I want you to know that when I met you...I knew you were everything I was looking for."

"Wait, what?" I finally realize she didn't see it yet. I need to keep her distracted now.

"I asked...what were you looking for in a mate? What was it about me?"

"Umm-- well, I--"

I hear a buzz. It's the door.

"Who is it?!" Angela asks, deeply frustrated.

"It's Agent Leigh," the freakishly loud voice answers, "I'm here to escort the two of you to see Sir Ruthven. He would like to have a word with the both of you."

"What about?" Angela sighs loudly.

"It's about the murder of Ivan Ruthven. You have ten seconds to open the door or I will break it down!"

I couldn't help but think: this might just be a case of out of the frying pan and into the fire...at least for one of us.

CHAPTER 20

Every step and every swing of my arms feels like a large magnetic pendulum-- counting down to the inevitable fate that awaits us. Agent Leigh looks up at me, I can see her in my peripheral vision but I don't return the glance. I know Angela is walking a few feet away from me but I won't look at her as long as I don't have to.

I've already tried to assess every possibility, every outcome. I've looked for every possible way to make it all work out for everybody somehow. Ultimately, I realized that there isn't anything worth worrying about anymore.

I have no illusions about this situation right now. There's only one possible outcome to this encounter with Sir Niklaus Ruthven, and there's absolutely nothing anyone can do about it.

As we enter the man's apartment, I think to myself that I can just calm down and relax now. There's nothing left to worry about, nothing left to put effort into. It's the final stretch of the race and I know exactly who comes out on top already.

I've seen, or at least read about, enough in this world to know that the good guys don't always win. I can accept that.

Angela and I take our seats across from Sir Ruthven as usual. It doesn't feel like a job interview to me this time, it just feels like destiny.

"Iryna's gone and betrayed your government, sir," Angela speaks out of turn. "She's responsible for the death of your brother, Ivan... and she's even conspiring with the son of Doctor Thornton. She is a damn traitor if there ever was one."

I stare at the wall behind Ruthven, in disbelief of my own poor judgment of character. How could I have trusted this girl with my life before? How could I not see what a disgusting, selfish animal she really is?

She embodies everything that is wrong with every dominant species this world has ever known... and I thought she would be my closest and most trusted friend for life.

"Agent Balmont," Ruthven says to me calmly, "do you have anything to add to this discussion?"

I sit in silence and don't bother to respond. For a long, silent stretch of ten seconds, Angela looks at me. At first, she smiles but then she begins to grow uncomfortable.

Maybe she thought I would say everything in my power to convince the man. Maybe she expected me to find every possible explanation in the world to turn the blame onto her.

Well she would be wrong.

I don't care. I have nothing more to add to the course of the universe. I am convinced that I know the outcome already, so what's the point?

I finally shake my head.

"Is that a no?" Ruthven asks me.

"That is a no." I smile calmly. "I have nothing more to add, sir."

Ruthven takes a deep breath and leans back on his chair. "Alright, ladies," he announces, "the two of you have an equal opportunity to prove that the other is in fact the guilty party."

Angela looks a bit disappointed. Maybe she expected him to convict and execute me then and there. Personally, I don't much care. I just lean back with the same level of comfort and look directly into the eyes of Niklaus Ruthven himself.

The leader continues, "Since, I presume, there is no physical evidence in this particular case, I will simply award the agent with the most probable and believable argument a victory. The guilty party will then be subject to whatever punishment is deemed appropriate by the victor. Is this understood?"

Angela nods with a satisfied smile.

I nod, knowing today is the day and none of us will change it now.

"I'll go first, if you don't mind." Angela says with a half-raised hand. She turns to me and asks with a smirk, "Is that okay with you, pretty girl?"

"Go right ahead, my love." I respond without giving her a moment of eye contact.

"Okay... You see, sir," Angela raises her tone proudly, "I have witnessed my friend, Iryna Balmont, murder a fellow member of the tribe. Following a psychology class with Professor Marsden, Iryna cold-heartedly lured a turned vampire into a target area by the forest and murdered the citizen in cold blood."

"Fascinating." Ruthven raises an eyebrow.

"Yeah... and then, on the mission, she decided to help Doctor Thornton and... well, she then threw your brother through the window of Thornton's bedroom."

"Did you try to aid my brother during this incident?"

"Uhh... Well... No." Angela's smile turns into a nervously distorted mouth. "I was knocked unconscious."

"So you did not witness the crime."

I sit silently...and so does Angela now.

Ruthven leans forward on his desk. "So, what you are telling me is that Agent Balmont decided, randomly, to murder my brother. And you simply know that Agent Balmont is responsible, but you did not witness it. Is this correct?"

Angela hesitates for a moment and shakily answers, "Well, yes... I woke up just in time to see her throw the table that sent it crashing out of the tower of Doctor Thornton's residence."

"Please repeat that. Did you just refer to my late brother as *it*?"

"Sorry," Angela chokes for a moment and recovers, "I meant to say he. Umm, I mean, him. She sent *him* crashing out of the tower."

Sir Ruthven glances at me for a moment. I maintain eye contact with no discernable expression. He looks at Angela again and takes a deep breath. He asks, "Angela... may I call you Angela?"

"Umm, yeah... Yes. Yes, of course, sir." Her face is gradually getting redder as she speaks.

"Angela, my good friend and collaborator, you say

that your fellow agent here had lured a member of the community into a target area. Is this correct?"

"Y... Yes, sir. She sure did, sir."

"Now, by what method exactly did she lure this turned vampire to be hunted?" He sips a glass of wine.

"What?" Angela hits a verbal roadblock for a moment. "I... don't understand the question."

"The question is very simple, Angela, my dear friend. By what means, do you claim, was used by the murderer to lure this vampire into the open?"

"Cookies, sir. She used cookies."

He takes a deep breath. "Do you consider me intelligent, Angela?"

Her eyes shoot open like headlights. "I'm sorry... I don't understand the question."

"Allow me to rephrase. Am I stupid to you?"

"No. No, you're not... sir." Her entire chair is vibrating from her shaky hands.

"Then why in the world do you expect me to forget the way in which we met?" He slams his hand on the table with a thundering crack.

Angela falls silent. She has no response.

Ruthven continues, "You say she lured the turned vampire into the target area with a cookie? Was this a, and I emphasize, turned vampire... such as myself, Donat, and my late brother, Ivan?"

"...Yes, but she..." Angela says as she chokes on her words.

"If I am not mistaken, Angela... It was you who hunted turned vampires using such a technique. Am I mistaken?"

"Yes... I mean, no... I mean, I really just..." Angela stumbles over her words. "But it was her! She's the one who's been talking to that Adrian kid. She's the one who killed your brother. You have to believe me!"

"I do not 'have to' do anything, my dear friend." He says in a calm and even voice. "You may be an experienced hunter, and you could have been of great use to our cause, but I am the leader of this region now... and you are a traitor to the administration of the United Tribes."

Ruthven slowly lights a cigar. He looks at me through the corner of his eye. He then glances at Angela... and back to me again.

"Do you have anything to add?" He finally questions me.

"Not really, sir. I have nothing at all to say." I answer without a hint of emotion.

Angela drops to her knees. "Please, Iryna. Please say something... Tell them what you did. Tell them the truth. Please! I'm begging you with everything I've got left in me... I love you."

I slowly turn to Angela and stare directly into her eyes. I take a deep breath and smile. Finally, I tell her, "You were right... You've already gotten what you came for, Angela. And you're finished."

She grabs my hand and I can feel her shaking like a motor. Tears run down her face like waterfalls. She's hysterical.

All the while, I have one thought in my mind: Remember what she did and how it felt. Remember it and know that this is what she had coming to her, in one way or another.

After a moment of silence, Ruthven reaches under his desk and presses a button.

"Agent Leigh," he calls out. "Come on in."

The short little, high-volume, agent enters. She must have been standing in the hallway on guard the whole time.

"At your service, sir," she says, loud and clear, as she stands perfectly upright.

"Execute her," Sir Ruthven orders in a calm voice.

"Sir... which one of them?" Agent Leigh asks.

"That one," he points directly at Angela.

She probably deserves anything that comes to her right now but a flood of guilt crashes into me like a brick wall. I can't let this happen--not like this.

Agent Leigh exposes her fangs with an enthusiastic smile that bevels her little cheeks. She slowly runs a sharpened fingernail down the side of Angela's neck. Blood drips from the fresh wound. With one hand, she tilts Angela's head over to the side, until her ear is snug against her shoulder and the open wound is stretched and exposed.

Leigh brings her fangs toward the wound to finish Angela off for good.

Sir Ruthven doesn't bother to watch. He just inhales from his cigar again.

"Stop this," I speak out. "*Please.* Stop this...sir."

Ruthven looks at me, either surprised at my courage or ready to confront my initial lack of respect. He raises a hand and Agent Leigh promptly stops dead in her tracks.

"Look at ourselves," I begin, "we are the new dominant species on the planet. We are the top of the food chain. We should be better than this."

"Agent Balmont," Ruthven responds, "I have already made my decision. I know that she is the guilty party. Do you know why?"

"But with all due respect, sir, you said that the

victor would decide the fate of the guilty party here, right?"

The man leans back on his chair. He grins. "I stand corrected, Agent Balmont. I admire your courage... What is your choice of punishment?"

"May I have a word with her first?"

He pauses for a moment and then nods. "You may."

I turn to Angela and gently wipe the tears from her cheeks.

"I just want you to know something," I whisper calmly and lovingly, "I actually enjoyed the first time we kissed. I enjoyed the first time we touched. I probably would have enjoyed the first time we were together. It all felt right... For the first time, it felt like true love.

"Ever since I was eight years old, I've been trying to find a mate in the city. I've always had this dream of finding someone... someone I could spend the rest of my life with. Every single time I see the inner city couples, hunting together, I get reminded of just how much I longed to be like one of them. They're beautiful to me. It doesn't matter what they look like or who they are. I just envy their trust in each other. I envy that feeling, just knowing someone will be there if the prey fights back, and knowing someone will be there if we develop the kinds of illnesses that the humans get."

Angela drops her eyes and looks down at the floor. I lift her head back up by her chin.

"See, Angela... I really did love you." I lean in closer. "And if you'd put your trust in me, your real trust... instead of trying to blackmail me just to fulfill your sexual desires... Well, we could've spent the rest of our lives together... forever."

I lean back on my chair.

Angela shakes and sobs, crying and growing beyond hysterical. Her face becomes a fountain of tears and saliva as she reaches out to lean her head on my arm.

I pull my arm away.

"P... please, Iryna." She pleads with a crackling voice. "Please don't leave me."

"It's too late," I answer coldly.

I turn to Ruthven. He probably has no idea what had just happened here but I'm sure he can see the depth of the pain in Angela's face.

After a long pause, he asks in a formal tone, "Alright, Agent Balmont. What is your choice of punishment?"

Angela and I walk quietly together, outside, toward the western clearing. This time, I'm leading the way--a first, come to think of it.

"Why'd you do that for me?" She asks. "Why would you let me go?"

"I wasn't done with you." I wink.

She laughs with a confidence that never seems to go away...even now.

We stop by the west end of the forest and look out onto the smog. It feels peaceful out here in the UV-filtered early morning sun. It actually looks a lot like I'd imagined it.

"What goes through your mind when you hurt people?" I ask her, out of the blue.

She chuckles at me. "I don't know what to say to that."

"I used to think we were all just trying to get by,

doing things the only way we know how. But what part of that makes you think you can just force yourself on people for your own pleasure? What part was smiling when you snapped all those turned vampires' necks?"

"I think you already know what you're wanting to say, girl. Why are you even asking me?"

"No, I really wanna know how your mind works. I used to think I understood, but I really don't."

She shakes her head and stares out into the distance without another word.

With one last breath, I ask her, "Are you at least sorry for what you did to Doctor Thornton?"

"Hell, no. Even if I regret everything else I ever done, I ain't about to regret that loser."

I pull her close and kiss her one last time in the filtered morning sunlight--a first and a last at once.

"I loved you," I tell her quietly. "I would have trusted you with my life but that wasn't enough."

She doesn't say a word. She just grins with a blatant arrogance as if I'd admitted to being a sucker to her scheming and manipulations...until she notices that Sara and Adrian are standing to either side of her.

"I'm not afraid of you anymore," Sara whispers to the now-straight-faced Angela. "I just pity you. You know how long I've been trying to make my so-called friends love me the way I loved them? You had that and you blew it...and for what? You know, it only took five minutes for Iry here to show me what having a real friend means. She helped me when she didn't have to and she made my day better even when hers was torn apart. Yet she loved you and you tore her heart to shreds. I'm not afraid of you anymore because there's nothing you can do to hurt me more than when you did that."

"What are you gonna do, shrimp, kill me?" Angela turns away from her with less confidence in her face than she attempts to fake.

Sara shrugs. "Why would I? I'm not the one whose father you murdered."

I look into Adrian's glistening eyes--immediately, I know and understand that he has it under control. Quietly, I turn and walk ten steps into the forest before I stop at a large tree trunk.

A loud snap rings through the air.

I cover my ears but it's too late. The sickening sound rings through my skull. I drop to the floor as a tear rolls down my cheek.

"Bye," I whisper quietly.

Adrian sits next to me and puts his arm around my shoulders as I look up at Sara.

"Sorry," he whispers quietly as he wipes the tear from my cheek.

"Don't be. She didn't deserve to be missed. My emotions are just stupid."

He pulls me closer. "I know, but no matter how we try to justify it, you just lost someone you loved too."

"She wasn't someone anyone deserves to have."

As I said before, there was only one possible outcome to this encounter, and there was absolutely nothing anyone could do about it.

The good guys didn't win--no one won. Adrian lost a father and I lost a friend. Angela was the best and the worst in more ways than one, but she was my first. I will never forget her.

CHAPTER 21

As I walk into Professor Marsden's lab, with a sense of personal closure, I find the professor lying flat on a hard, metallic table top. She doesn't seem to be breathing. In fact, she's not moving at all as far as I can tell.

I freeze. It couldn't be. Not now. Not ever. I came to say goodbye, but not like this. Slowly, I approach her body and carefully observe her face. She looks cold and pale. I walk closer--

"Iryna!" She pops up and stares at me straight in the eyes.

I jump two feet in the air. My arms feel tingly and my heart feels like it just dropped to the floor.

She laughs and rubs her eyes. "Sorry, dear. I was just taking a nap. Teaching the likes of you is a stressful full-time acting job. I needed a little entertainment."

"Don't scare me like that! I thought you were--"

"Dead? No, Iryna. I will not leave you alone so soon... I will nag you with my theories until you-- Wait. That odor on you..."

"What? Blood?"

"No, dear. I would recognize your blood... It is a distinct chemical, one that I have studied and..." Suddenly, her eyes seem to shoot wide open, fully awakened by some discovery, or a shock. "Iryna! Have you been abusing Scarbromine against my warnings?"

I step back. "No, why?"

"Do not lie to me, dear. Tell me the truth. I would recognize the scent anywhere. It is not a substance to be toyed with."

"No, I really didn't. I never even-- Umm, did you just say horse radish?"

She hops off the table and jogs clumsily to a cupboard. "Yes... There is a distinct odor that is likened to horse radish. As a user, you should be accustomed to it."

I stand rigidly. "Professor, I think I've been drugged...more than once."

She scrounges through a metal box and retrieves a syringe. "How do you mean... drugged?" Then she dashes to me and prepares the needle.

"I think Angela used that stuff on me to knock me out... I had a recurring dream, and it was the same one I had at the apartment. And I also smelled horse radish there, so maybe there were addicts in the area who--"

She jabs the needle into my neck. "These dreams, were they memories?"

"Ow! Well, I don't know, I thought maybe it was just a recurring nightmare getting more and more vivid, but then Sara told me about the Blonde Butcher and I started to suspect that maybe my--"

"It is possible that your continued exposure to

Scarbromine, even to the scent of it, may cause you to recall your first exposure to the narcotic. A recall of the first exposure is a very commonly known side effect of Scarbromine abuse. It is the reason many of the youths of your generation overdose on it the moment before a planned loss of their virginity."

"Are you telling me these dreams could be real? That they really happened?"

"Are you truly so surprised, dear?"

"... No. Not really," I confess. "I think a part of me just wishes it was nothing but a hallucination."

"Often times, these recalled memories will have a certain familiarity to them. There is a marked difference between hallucinations and memories. This is one of the rare cases in which I would place any credibility in the retrieval of repressed memories."

"You don't think that happens all the time?"

"Occasionally...but not often. However, for a vampire with a history of repeated Scarbromine exposure, I believe it is possible that you have retrieved a lost memory...if, indeed, you experienced a sense of familiarity, that is." She puts the syringe away.

"Yeah, I did." I rub the soreness on my neck. "So what'd you just give me anyway?"

"It is a chemical that I have tested to reduce the risk of addiction from prolonged, repeated exposure to Scarbromine. I had intended to administer it to you sooner, but we have all been sidetracked of late, as I am sure you would understand." She puts the metal box back into the cupboard. "What, may I ask, were these dreams about?"

"My family. Up until now, I was convinced that my

family was robbed. I'm not even so sure that's what Valeska meant to tell me--I think it's just how I took it."

"Valeska Balmont..."

"Yeah, she was my twin sister...or *is*, I guess. And I think she's the one they call the Blonde Butcher."

After we say our goodbyes, I realize that the professor has been a guide to me in so many ways. The truth is I'd hoped she would agree to come with us but she insists on staying to finish the semester of her class. She promised we'll meet up again under better circumstances but she just wants to finish what she started here.

For me to finish what I had started, it's time to go back to the East Coast and make up for the wrongs I had been a part of here.

I arrive at the train station and it's about nine o'clock in the morning. Nine is just around the typical bed time for many of the adults of our species. It's late enough for sunrise but early enough that I'd left a few hours to wait before the train arrives.

By ten o'clock, I notice more and more people joining me on the ramp for the train heading to the East Coast. I recognize a few of the other students from my class, but I don't know any of them by name. I also have no idea who's really coming with us, and who's just visiting a friend or a relative in the Eastern regions.

I try to keep to myself.

After all, we're trying to escape one of the most carelessly destructive leaders this world has known for decades. Maybe he's got spies and security staff watching all the public transportation areas.

It'd be much more comforting knowing someone I'm on speaking terms with is waiting here with me but I don't see anyone yet.

Silently staring at the tracks, I begin to imagine that these tracks lead straight to the city where I raised myself.

I'm amazed that memories of the East Coast are actually becoming nostalgic to me now. When I lived there all those years, it was just the background setting of my every-day life. There was nothing special about it even if millions of human tourists came to visit it as the highlight of a vacation. To me, it was never anything special. But today, my trip back home feels like an act of reclaiming my freedom from all the reminders of a certain former friend.

Another half hour passes...

Adrian arrives.

He smiles as soon as he sees me and moves closer. "Hey, before we go, I think I should tell you something."

I just smile back in silence--pretty much knowing exactly what he's about to say.

He continues, "I wasn't always a vampire. I was--"

"Turned," I finish his sentence for him. "I know. I never forgot about you since the day we first met. I never knew anyone who cared as much as I do about the animals."

Adrian falls into a dead silence. His eyes glisten in the filtered sunlight--the shine of his light blue iris shines more beautifully than even the first time I had seen them.

I move closer and whisper, "Do you trust me?"

He nods and smiles. My pulse begins to speed up.

He tilts his head to expose his neck and I offer him my wrist.

Our fangs gently press into each other's bare skin...until it breaks and warm blood bubbles out of our fresh wounds. Slowly, carefully, we draw blood from each other, tiny bits at a time to be sure not to hurt each other.

A tiny little hand taps on my shoulder.

It's Sara.

She gets wrapped in the tightest Iry-Sara hug sandwich that I could possibly manage.

Everything about her tells me she wants to be close with me as much as I'd want to be with her. Even that nickname actually sounds adorable to me now, surprisingly--I guess it's starting to grow on me. Too bad I can't really make her name any shorter.

I look down and see that her leg is wrapped in a makeshift bandage. It looks more like a ripped piece of table cloth tied into a ragged bundle of knots.

"It's mostly healed now, it just looks all leathery and rough so I wanna cover it up for a bit," she explains. "I found out what you did for me by the way, smarty pants."

At eleven o'clock in the morning, the train arrives and unloads a seemingly endless stream of passengers from other cities before we're allowed to board.

After we take our seats in the train, it feels like the beginning of a new life is right at the tips of our fingers but not quite within reach.

Somehow, I feel like I was meant to travel all this way, just to meet a few people that I could trust, and then bring them back home with me to start a new life. The professor would probably tell me that it's a subjective idea formed in my own head to relieve responsibility for my own choices, and she'd probably be right. I feel better believing that it all makes sense in the end. Maybe that's all that matters for me.

It's time for us all to take the front seat in our own lives now.

The old world is gone but a lot of its influence and its shortcomings are still there. I used to believe vampire nature will never change--but all we can do is try.

Unfortunately, not everyone shares this ideal.

Agent Leigh and three others in uniform approach the closed doors of the train.

"Do you think he sent them to stop us?" Sara whispers.

I shrug but decide not to take any chances. We lower ourselves and lean back on our seats.

Out of curiosity, I peak at Leigh and the others again. It looks like they're arguing with a young vampire wearing an old human train company uniform. I don't have a clue what they're saying except for the fact that Leigh's loud voice allows me to hear a few vowels here and there--even through the glass of the train's windows. It's not enough to tell if they're talking about us.

Finally, the train leaves the station as Leigh and her squad members watch. Adrian, Sara and I glance at each other with a collective sigh of relief.

Suddenly, Adrian taps me on my shoulder. "Hey, why's that little human over there staring at you like that?"

Slowly and cautiously, I stick my head out into the isle.

It's that little dark-haired human girl... the one who stabbed me in the back, the day I met the professor. She's sitting by herself on the last seat of the car.

I figure she's been following me around for a while now... Maybe it's time to find out why.

I stand up off my seat and slowly walk toward her.

Everyone watches me. Who knows what they're thinking. I just know that little child has guts, sitting in a train full of our kind all by herself.

Adrian grabs my arm and makes me jump. "You want me to come with you?" he whispers.

I shrug. "Don't worry about it... It's just a human girl. It's not like she can bite me."

Carefully, I approach the little girl and take a seat next to her. "Why are you following me?"

She doesn't answer at first.

Something about her chills me to my core. Maybe it's because I'm finally noticing her wise-beyond-her-years aura. I try my best not to make any sudden, alarming movements around her... as if her vision were based on movement.

I can see her entire body bounce up in the air when the train runs over a bump on the tracks, but I know she's a tough little human.

Finally, she looks up at me. "Relax," she says in a soft voice. "I won't hurt you again."

I never thought I would hear those words coming from a human. Then again, stranger things have happened that I never thought possible.

She asks, "Have you found her yet?"

I turn to look at her. "Found who?"

"Your sister."

"How'd you know she was my sister?"

"I *do* know how to get answers out of people." With a wink, she holds a pocket open to reveal the handle of the dagger she had stabbed me with before.

"What's your name?" I ask with a nervous and quivering smile. "You never told me your name."

"It's not important."

I lean in and whisper, "Okay, '*not important*'... So you thought I was her at first, right? When you broke free and got the knife back, why didn't you try to kill me then? How did you know I wasn't her two minutes later?"

She turns away. "'Cause I saw your eyes...I'll never forget her eyes."

"Well, whatever she did to you...I'm sorry."

"You didn't do anything bad. Valeska did. And I know she's not sorry for it. I saw it in her eyes. She enjoyed it and so will I."

We sit quietly and look out the window together.

I finally ask, "So...what would you do...if I really were my sister--if I really were Valeska Balmont?"

Calm and distant, she answers, "I'd cut your blood-dripping heart out, slowly, and smile...just like Valeska did to my family."

I squeeze right in between Sara and Adrian on the train seat. We lean on each other for hours as we watch the scenery through the windows, in broad UV-filtered daylight, for the first time in our lives. It may not be as beautiful as the clear skies the humans once saw, but it's the most beautiful sight anyone in our species has had the chance to witness.

"Hey... There's something I've always wanted to do," I tell them with a smile worthy of a five year old on Christmas Eve. "Give me your hands."

Gently, I run my sharpened fingernail down Adrian's palm. Blood slowly spreads onto his handprint.

"You too," I tell Sara. "Are you ready?"

She nods. "Yeah. I'm from the East Coast too, remember?" Her eyes look deep into mine with her lower lids arched in an undeniably beautiful smile as I bleed her palm.

And then I bleed both of my own palms. "Okay, this is it." I clasp onto Adrian's and Sara's hands.

I close my eyes and whisper the words I've wanted to say for years, "I've been waiting my whole life for you."

On our journey back to the East Coast, Adrian plans to help re-structure the governments and eventually impact the lives of millions. The way I see it, whether we succeed or not, we're a family now. That's what matters.

For the rest of the train ride, Sara, Adrian and I share our experiences in the West Coast and, in each of our own ways, learn a little more about what it's like to be in different shoes on the same path.

By two in the afternoon, we fall asleep with their heads on each of my shoulders, as our pale skin reflects the filtered sunlight that shines in through open blinds.

Aside from bathing in sunlight, I've seen and experienced a lot lately that I never even thought possible. I stepped out of my comfort in misery and found new forms of lies, deceit, and pain...but on that same road, I found my first taste of love, trust, and purpose.

Maybe now, I can help the rest of the world do the same.

It's an understatement to say that things have changed in the world around us. In many ways, I still identify with humanity more readily than I do with my own species--after all, I grew up among them and continue to mourn the fall of their civilization. As Adrian, Sara, and I navigate the former state of New York, we settle in by the water falls once recognized as the border between the human nations of the United States and Canada.

Adrian tells me that the lights of Clifton Hill illuminated the Canadian side for decades--the dark ruins we stand before is only a shadow of its former glory.

Over the following months, we meet a group of fellow vampire survivors working to rebuild the former Niagara region into a haven for vampires with a vision of a bright new world on the surface. As I prepare to hand these volumes to a self-designated courier, I address it to Professor Marsden and look up at the filtered light.

You could say it was fate...but I believe choices brought us here. And maybe that's all that matters.

VISIT US

AT

www.VampireAge.com

FOR

UPDATES & PROMOTIONS

www.ingramcontent.com/pod-product-compliance
Lightning Source LLC
Chambersburg PA
CBHW050029180626
46810CB00002B/642